COLLAPSIBLE

Other books by Tim Conley

Whatever Happens
Nothing Could Be Further
One False Move
Dance Moves of the Near Future

COLLAPSIBLE

TIM CONLEY

New Star Books • Vancouver • 2019

NEW STAR BOOKS LTD.
107 – 3477 Commercial Street, Vancouver, BC V5N 4E8   CANADA
1574 Gulf Road, No. 1517, Point Roberts, WA 98281   USA
www.NewStarBooks.com ◆ info@NewStarBooks.com

The publisher acknowledges the financial support of the Canada Council
for the Arts and the British Columbia Arts Council.

Canada Council   Conseil des arts
for the Arts   du Canada

BRITISH COLUMBIA
ARTS COUNCIL
An agency of the Province of British Columbia

Cataloguing information for this book is available from Library and
Archives Canada, www.collectionscanada.gc.ca.

Cover design by Robin Mitchell Cranfield
Printed and bound in Canada by Imprimerie Gauvin, Gatineau, QC
First published February 2019

for Gail and Julian

Those who make a practice of comparing human actions are never so perplexed as when they try to see them as a whole and in the same light; for they commonly contradict each other so strangely that it seems impossible that they have come from the same shop.

— Montaigne

TABLE OF CONTENTS

ENANTIODROMIA
OR SOMETHING LIKE IT

The world's foremost authority on werewolves is buying a new suit. This is a rare occasion but he acts unsurprised and the tailor moving softly about him knows better than to remark on his customer's misunderstandings of his gentle questions. A conference, the occasion turns out to be, an invitation to a select international conference. The gentleman will want to remember to undo the jacket when he sits, after delivering his address, of course. A shadow crosses the customer's face, and when it passes he agrees, yes, after delivering my address. In fact he has not considered that he might very well be expected to make some sort of speech — the invitation did not mention it, but certainly it seems a possibility, even a likelihood.

— If you would raise your arms just so, says the tailor, and hold them like that for just a few moments.

He does so, and thinks again about his ex wife, again about whether it would be better to inform her of this honour, this expenses-paid trip to Geneva, this recognition of his years of painstaking research, or to keep it secret from her, at least for now, maybe even for as long as it takes for her to learn of it from some other source, such as the mass media. He is no more able to decide now than he was yesterday, when the invitation arrived.

What sort of speech would be expected of him, he wonders as he pays the tailor, pays with money that would otherwise go to his ex-wife, she of little faith. It will be ready at the end of the week, the tailor assures him, but the world's foremost authority on werewolves, recently addressed as such in a remarkable invitation, is out the door with excited, troubled thoughts. He can imagine himself rising from a table, unbuttoning no buttoning the jacket to his new suit as he does so, and addressing the assembled experts. He can see it all very clearly in his mind, especially now that he knows what the suit will look like, but he cannot hear anything, cannot make out what he is so confidently and suavely saying.

At the snap of five o'clock the tailor closes his shop, the shop that his father had opened and worked in for nearly half a century, and puts everything in order. On the floor he finds a business card, which must have fallen from someone's pocket. There was only one fitting that day, so there's no mystery there, but he is puzzled by a word on the card: *Lycanthropologist*. He says it aloud, slowly, and though it sounds even more impressive than it looks, it is no clearer to him. He takes the card home with the intention of showing it to his daughter.

Deja is at the moment he arrives home making chili for dinner. This kind of activity is a definite sign that she is in good spirits, but, it is terrible to admit even to himself, he is usually suspicious at these moments. Of course he is immensely glad to see her get the upper hand on the depression that so often has her in a fierce hold, to the point that she stays abed bundled thick in blankets on the hottest summer days, complaining of a cutting wind no one else can feel, and those are not the worst days. Of course he is glad to see her hopping around the little kitchen in the apartment they share, taking care to make a meal that they can share. How many times, however, has he found her animated in this way for reasons that were anything but assuring?

She brings him a taste of the chili on a wooden spoon, and they agree as they always have that this is what wooden spoons are for: to let one person give another a taste of something. It would not do to eat an entire meal with a wooden spoon, that special implement for stirring and sampling. The origins of this joke between them, spoony banter, are lost to both of their memories, but still they carry on, a kind of stirring.

— Deja, I wanted to ask you, do you know what this word means, oh now I've forgotten it. Hang on, let me find that card.

His hands, precise, she watches, check here and check there, discover, transfer to hers.

— This is a new word to me, she says, wrinkling her nose, but I can guess what it means. Is this one of your clients?

— Yes, a new one. He came in today and ordered a new suit. But I was hoping that perhaps you could tell me what it means, *lycan* what is it, *lycanthopolotrist.*

Her laughter is undoubtedly his favourite sound, the reason he wants never to lose his hearing.

— Lycanthropologist.

The chili is excellent, the bread is fresh. With dancing hands Deja explains that she has discovered a new bakery, down a little street that anyone can miss. Both she and her father must have walked by it any number of times without noticing it, but early this morning it was the magnificent smell that led her to turn where she had never turned before. A newly painted but modest sign announced a bakery, without further information. Inside two small women with bright teeth were delighted to greet her, to sell her the bread, to give her a packet of miguelitos free of charge, which Deja and her father would be having for dessert.

Dessert! The tailor smiles but is on guard: this may be going too far, an excess that indicates a problem, an over-doing of things. His wife, rest her soul, was always so much better at these things: so much more perceptive, so much surer in knowing the way to handle them.

— They were both speckled with flour, both with sing-song voices, and those identical crooked noses. I asked if they were sisters and they laughed, for they are apparently asked that all the time, but all the same their laughter was so genuine. They told me that they met a few years ago on a holiday, amazed to meet someone else so alike. And they discovered that both of them had always dreamed of open-ing a little bakery.

It is a sweet story, the tailor and his daughter agree as they eat their dessert, but there is more to the story than they know. There is a man lurking in the story, an admirer who cannot make up his mind which of the two women he wants to propose to, though he is determined to marry one of them. They have noticed him lurking, looking and not looking, as he has been inexpertly doing for months now, even before the bakery opened. He is unmistakable, for he has a crooked nose and a nervous habit of scratching it, as though to make it disappear. One of the bakers thinks him somewhat amusing, the other thinks him somewhat sinister, and it is one of the few disagreements between them. It goes without saying that neither of them has any thought of marrying him, for they have each other and their bakery.

Their admirer is no genius, no millionaire, and thanks to his nose, not much of a looker: he knows all of this, he admits this to himself. His voice is not very pleasant. He also has no luck and little experience with or understanding of women. His prospects are incontestably few. But, rightly or wrongly, he prides himself on his patience.

— Circumstances change, he says to himself from time to time. Children in the market square watch for him every week, the man who talks to himself this way. They do not quite dare to approach him directly, but they have sometimes rushed by him in a giggling mass, almost tripping him up. They crack each other up by twisting their noses and muttering, skulking about.

The best imitation is Esteban's: this is the unanimous view. At nearly eight years of age Esteban also does very good imitations of the doctor with the limp, a couple of crosseyed priests, and the stepmother of one of his friends, a woman on whom they all have a hopeless, unutterable crush. A gifted mimic, his grandmother's assessment, may not be entirely praise. Hers is the only authority that Esteban acknowledges, for he knows that she sees through everyone, and there is no fooling the old woman who has seen and survived as many marriages as wars. Never would Esteban dare even to attempt to imitate her sidelong glances, her pointing to a heaven that she denied was there, her little pouts. There was a certain manner in which she would set down her cup of tea or the book she was reading onto a table so as to announce that what she was about to say next required much of her and thus even more of her listener.

Many times she told her grandson about her sister, long dead, and her sister's firmly held view that life is chiefly composed of hallucinations. Not in the Berkeleyan sense, she explained, without stooping to define such terms to the boy. There were real phenomena, or real enough not to merit splitting hairs over, death and pain and hunger the usual and ungainsayable examples. Her sister believed that human relations were the central hallucinations of our lives.

— You think you know me but you do not. I think I know you or our father or the policeman across the street but I do not. You are as much a figment of my imagination as I am of yours. Not that I like you any the less for that, of course. Hallucinations can be very engaging.

— You're only saying this to keep distance between us, between yourself and other people. You're only saying these things because you're afraid of getting hurt.

— You misunderstand me. I am talking about a dissolving of distance and difference. As I conjure you up, make you real to me, I become you.

— I don't understand.

— It's not too much to say that we dream one another, her sister said, in a voice of softest resignation, a gentle animal going to sleep.

Now the grandmother dreams of her grandson, whom she loves. He is clever but lacks guidance, but he cannot be some hallucination of hers: she will not accept that. From the window she sees him running into an open pipe — is it a construction yard? When he does not emerge she calls his name: Esteban, Esteban. But her voice is weak and she is unable to open the heavy window.

Esteban, Esteban. The echoes in the pipe, the echoes in the pipe. First he shouts his own name, then those of his friends, saving the names of the two girls till last, then the name of his friend's stepmother, and then, more nervously, a few expletives, the worst ones he has heard but never before had a chance or the nerve to utter. Though he has to crouch a little inside the pipe, with his feet spread apart and his hands pressed against the side he can make the whole thing roll back and forth just a little, emboldening him to shout the most vicious words more loudly, and then release a full-throated howl. The pipe rolls more to the right than expected and it occurs to him that it might roll further. It may be his own temerity at this moment shocks him, but in any event he makes to run out of the pipe, but bashes his face against this side and then the next on his way out, and he cannot tell if the pipe is rolling out of control or if it is just him.

When he emerges is gasping and finds bright blood on his shirt. He gradually stands up straight and scratches his nose, remembering that he has damaged it. There are things we have to live with, he thinks. That's just the way thing are, but things change.

— Circumstances change, he says, listening to how different, how older his voice sounds to him now.

All this construction — what are they building? The town keeps developing.

— Circumstances change. He hears the sound of children giggling, turns, and sees a blur of them fly down a side street. He peers around this corner and a third of his senses comes to the fore: the fragrance of fresh bread. The bakery is opening. A woman, small and toothy with her arms covered in flour, turns a crank to raise an awning above the storefront. She can tell that it will not rain today, simply by sniffing the air. The air tells her everything: she and the atmosphere are on very good terms.

She will not be convinced otherwise. The limping doctor and his lackeys can think what they like. She knows when it will rain, and she is not alone. Her other self is here now, kneading flour, anticipating how tried she will be at day's end when, at the snap of five o'clock, they close the bakery and walk home, past the apartment building that is slowly rising higher than any of the other buildings in town. Making bread is a way of healing, she told the doctor. They both of them told the doctor that. And the doctor offers no explanation for the blockhead with the crooked nose always sniffing after them, neither threat nor fool, only a persistence.

— How long did you say that you have had this shop here? this customer is asking.

— I didn't say, she answers as she wraps the bread. You must have been speaking with my business partner. We own the bakery together. We are so alike that we are often mistaken for one another.

The amazed customer, a young woman with short hair, says that they must be sisters.

She laughs. She hands the young woman a packet of miguelitos.

— On the house.

Deja strolls past the fountain where the market square used to be. With some distaste she enters the air-conditioned grocery store down the street from her apartment building, no longer strolling but on a kind of shopper's march, and buys the few vegetables she needs for dinner. Reminding herself of the miguelitos and the surprise for her father buoys her through waiting in line and the almost wordless exchange with the cashier. And now she is out again in the open air, a light sailing breeze rather than a cold wind.

She is adapting her mother's recipe, a risky variation. As the smell of chili begins to fill the apartment, she grows more confident, and thinks of her mother's sure hand stirring as her own stirs the wooden spoon. The wooden spoon is a relay baton of sensation, a device of transference. Deja is almost dancing in front of the stove. All at once she knows that she is going to write a poem about this spoon, and the realization excites her like the best news.

This news has to be held back when her father arrives, for she can see that he is in poor spirits from the way that he tries to conceal that fact. Depression seldom has any claim on him, and she is generally more familiar with it than he and so quick to spot it. A bad day at work? She leads him to a chair and lets him take a taste from the wooden spoon. The chili pleases him, make him more communicative, and she kisses his forehead. A bad day, yes, a discouraging day. A customer came to return a suit, demanding a full refund, a suit for which he had been fitted, asking even for his deposit back. With his characteristic calm the tailor pointed out that that was not possible: the suit was custom-tailored, and as he had told the gentleman during the final fitting, the day before he left for Geneva, that some repairs would be possible but no refunds. First the customer snorted and stomped about, derision sliding into rage. He raved incoherently about customer service, about years of painstaking research, about the treachery of pranksters, about imaginary international conferences meant to divert and humiliate him, about who knows what, to the point that the tailor grew alarmed that the man was transforming before his eyes into some sort of wild beast, and for a few moments he contemplated calling the police. Eventually, however, the customer's frenzy waned and on his knees he began weeping.

— What did you do, papa?

He helped the man to stand up, eased him out of his coat, and stepped away from him a moment. He returned with the jacket of his suit, which he helped the customer put on, and told him what a fine choice he had made, how good it looked.

— And I told him that the suit was his, and that without a doubt he would have before long an occasion to wear it, perhaps some other international conference, for there are always more international conferences, aren't there?

But the world's foremost authority on werewolves would not stop crying. His expenses would not be reimbursed after all. His ex-wife, having gotten wind of his extravagance, has unleashed her lawyer. His tears were pooling on the floor of the tailor's shop, the same floor that his father had walked on, measuring suits for gentlemen for nearly half a century.

— So I gave him his money back.

— All of it?

He nods glumly but she embraces him. According to her, he is the kindest man. According to him, he is a foolish man quickly being consigned to the past. She serves the chili and watches him worry. Just wait until she tells him about dessert!

AFTER SCHOOL SPECIAL

All parking lots are sad but some are sadder than others. The parking lot in front of the beer store, for instance, has seen a lot of trouble, would like to become indifferent, truly indifferent, but cannot. The hospital parking lot has absorbed grief, so much grief that it can absorb nothing else: this is its only diet. So the parking lots of the various banks know only the taste of disappointment, and would savour it, if they could; so the parking lots of abandoned arenas and shabby motels and police stations and advertising agencies can only be sad, different gradations of sad. Neither bio nor sphere, they are kissed only by cigarettes, congregationalist flyers, divorced chopsticks, and broken bodies of seagulls. The parking lots offer nothing in return but sorrow in generous proportions.

But it wasn't always this way. When the ancient Greeks poured the first concrete, there was love in it, joy, compassion. The ancient Greeks were named Brad and Georgina. It is said that at their wedding, the sacrifice of scores of seagulls to honour the gods (with a special nod to Apollo the charioteer) made the sun flash once, warmly, as it set. The mixture they wrought had absorbed their happiness, and spread out over the soil with a sense of harmony. Those who parked there, when at last cars were invented, felt inexplicably reassured, as if given a kind of telluric pat on the back: everything is going to be just fine.

How, when did this dramatic change come about? Was it chemical? Alchemical? Metaphysical? One herpatologist with a drinking problem has speculated that a passing comet's methane might have possessed some emotionally disruptive effects, and was passively sopped up by the parking lots. This is surely wrong. But what of theories about industrial pollution, time distortion, continental drift, ambient ressentiment, spontaneous artificial intelligence, necromancy?

Might as well ask Alison, who has parked in front of Liberty Bowl for almost fifteen years now. She used to work there, under the original owners, but stopped getting out of her car to come in. "My world is everything that's in the car," she reports. "Fsthsthsthsthhh." The last is a sound that she often makes that no one is certain is a titter. Her rear window is entirely obscured by the detritus that consumes all the interior space save the driver's seat. Through the windows can be made out plastic bags, styrofoam cartons, stuffed toys, bike chains, issues of *Yachting Enthusiast*, legal pads filled with pencilled numbers, other carbon-based stuff. "Too much movement damages the aether. No one takes the bottles, no one takes the bottles. There is only the one true god." Poor Alison, her hair tied in knots to keep it from her eyes. "The future unpacks its own suitcase. Keep your chewing gum away from me." Is your life one of depression caused by the psychometry of the parking lot, or have you dedicated yourself to studying or even assuaging the suffering palpable in this liminal space or non-space? "Fsthsth. Fsthsthsthsthtsh."

Released from school, children cross the parking lot and talk and tease. They have muddled ideas about sex and radiation. There once was a woman who lived in a Ford. She would tell them how sad their lives will be but they talk and tease. "God is a seagull," she says. "A miserable unforgiving seagull."

BEHIND THE SCENES

Kowai mono mitasa.
— Japanese proverb

Just before the salads came she noticed that he had something up his nose. The left nostril (his left), something solid. She leaned a little closer while he was telling her about how he had gone to university to study sports management but to appease his father he took a minor in business and that decision turned out to get him the job at the bank. She tried to lean in such a way that might suggest attentiveness rather than anything more, eating her salad and trying to get a better look at the thing up his nose. It was solid and, she thought, inorganic. She was fairly certain it hadn't been there earlier. Now he was talking about salads, because he could see that she was enjoying her salad, and didn't she think that salads were always great when someone else made them for you, but only when someone else made them? She nodded but he pressed on: did she know what the best thing about working in the bank was? (She remembered how Chiyo insisted on paying for their coffees as she admitted, well, he works in a bank, and Kiwa repeated, he works in a bank, and Chiyo tried to laugh it off, saying, it's a job, that has to count for something, and Kiwa said, counting is the operative word.) No, she really did not know what the best thing about working in a bank was. It gives you, he said, excitedly trying to figure out how to end his sentence, it gives you a look behind the scenes.

When he was telling her that he had taken over his father's investment portfolio and really made something of it, Kiwa determined that the object was metallic, a greyish blue. And when he was telling her that even his uncle, who had, as a matter of fact, always dismissed his nephew as a fool, had now not only recanted but repeatedly asked him for some financial advice, she thought that she could see some sort of writing on the metallic object up his nose, though whether it was lettering or numbering the restaurant lighting refused to let her discover. Could she take him after dinner to her apartment and find him a seating position next to a strong lamp? She found herself seriously exploring the question. After all (she told herself), most of the men she had taken back to her apartment in the past couple of years had been taken out of curiosity, one way or another. She took a deep gulp of wine and he remarked that the wine was good.

She decided to let him decide. (There's a cold streak in you, Chiyo liked to say, with equal parts amusement and admiration.) She suggested that there must be a lot of risk involved in the kind of banking he did, and she could see him trying to balance the urge to reassure her of his utter competence, not to lay too fine a point on it, and thus play down the element of risk, and the contrary urge to acknowledge what might be a compliment, a projected image of him as a man who savours the thrill of risk. It quickly became apparent that this tightrope act was too much for him. He swayed from one tack to another: a testy distinction between the solidity of the system and the fatal lack of conviction shared by some timorous elements within the system; then a concession that the system might be improved, of course, and that banking evolves as an economy changes, like a living thing; then an apology-question hybrid seeking assurance that he was not boring her with so technical a subject; but before she could reply, had she wanted to, he denounced Chinese communism which incidentally was a very good example of how the free market prevails in the end; then he started to tell a story about a time he had stood up to or gotten the better of or barely escaped from a gang of Chinese thugs, but his doubts about its relevance slowly brought him to a stop. After a moment of looking at it fiercely, he slurped his glass empty and refilled it.

Kiwa knew that she could say nothing, that he would probably now become aloof or resentful after having letting her see such a fumble. (The wisdom of Chiyo: men without women are men unsure of themselves. And here I am supposed to be the one with the cold streak, Kiwa replied.) She was not going to let go of her mystery just yet. The server came to tempt them with dessert — she pretended to think that tiramisu was an everyday word she could not place, but the server corrected her before her date could, so she asked the server for some time to consider, and considered instead how to save the banker some face without knowing for certain why she was doing so.

My grandfather, she said, was ninety-two years old when he passed away last year. The banker, silent since his saga of the Chinese gang petered out, blinked and waited for more, undoubtedly waiting to see what this new topic had to do with him. My mother's father, she said, and slid hair from her bare shoulder that had not been bothering her in the slightest. It is hard to believe that he's gone. The banker said that he was sorry to hear it: had they been close? He lived with us for some of the years I was growing up, she explained, and sometimes he could be kind, very kind, and he was quiet and gentle, but he was very disapproving of so many things. Even though he would say nothing, everyone could feel his disapproval in the air, you couldn't miss it. He would disapprove of this. Of what? Of the whole situation: eating in an "Italian" restaurant, dinner alone with a stranger, this dress. At last the banker took up his role: though we owe great respect to our elders, this is a new age, a new country. For example, he bet that her grandfather disapproved of the internet. She laughed, he did, he did, and brushed that hair from her shoulder again.

It dawned on her then, as she got another half-decent look at the thing up the banker's nose, why she should find herself thinking about her grandfather at this moment: his models. Nothing so fully absorbed the old man than meticulously painting his diecast models of warplanes. The more detail required, the greater concentration and more time required, the prouder he would ultimately be of his accomplishment, a pride that could be measured by the discerning observer by how modest he became when it was noticed. Very tiny numbers, historically correct designations, always perfectly written — as though stencilled, though of course it was all by untrembling free hand — on the sides of those little planes. It could not be a model warplane up his nose, of course, for the size and shape were all wrong, but now it was hard not to see the inscription as numerical designation of some kind, and she decided that she would not have dessert, thank you all the same, and that she was going to ask: what do you say to a glass of wine at my place?

He paid with a golden credit card that she was meant to notice and as she passed through the door he held open she glanced back to see whether the angle and the change in lighting helped make out what that thing was when she tripped and scraped her knee on the sidewalk. The banker was gallant but began talking about the possibility of infection in a cut, even a simple scrape like that one; she winced less from the little pain in the knee than from her inability to see a way not only to interrupt but to extend the invitation and make it plausible. He had an idea — she knew this because he told her he had an idea, and waited for her to ask what it was. Do you know The Midnight Whistle? he asked. It's a nightclub, not far from here, we can go for a drink there and get your knee cleaned and bandaged. He reiterated the dangers of infection as he hailed a taxi. She did not protest. She got into the taxi and imagined herself telling Chiyo the next day: my knee hurt, your friend's friend is way too much of an amateur epidemiologist, but I was determined to find out what that thing was up his nose.

The taxi went east within Shinjuku, the driver talking with the banker about traffic conditions the whole way. The words Midnight Whistle were lit in lavender and even before entering she could tell that without question it was a gay club. Kiwa felt her plans drop out of reach as they stepped inside: the only lights were the blue glow of the bar and itinerant flashes of cellphones. A beefy DJ in a sleeveless tuxedo, ducking out of one set of headphones into another, was doing something with police sirens, a skipping base beat, and Cat Stevens hoping you make a lot of nice friends out there. The banker steered her to the corner of the bar. Do you come here often? she asked. He grinned: as a matter of fact, he recently became one of the owners of the building. Did he own many buildings? she dutifully asked and rubbed her knee. He obtained a clean cloth from one of the bartenders and handed it to her as he shared with her the confidential fact that he owned a few. She probably thought it was expensive, and she would be right. But as a matter of fact, he said, and here the music rendered several words inaudible, then something about a terrible slump with no good projections for the future. Something after that and then something about the bubble economy of a dozen years ago were going to be felt for a long time to come. We have to start thinking differently, he concluded. What would you like to drink?

He recommended something and she sipped it: cold and sweet, difficult to say just how potent. Almost all of the customers were men, as far as she could judge; the bartenders were a blurrier blend. Bad and beware, Cat Stevens was stammering, bad and beware. She did not like clubs and tried to show it discreetly, but turned to see the banker, whose name she realized she could not remember, downing a small row of brightly coloured shots and getting cheered on by a few guys at the bar. She looked carefully at them but saw nothing protruding from any nostrils. Nor did they seem to notice anything sticking out of his nose, but then even she could only just see it and she was standing next to him. How's your knee? All right, she said, but thought to add: it would help if I could sit down somewhere for a few minutes. Hang on, he said. He got a beer from the bar, took her hand, and led her slowly through the jostling bodies to a staircase at the back. She saw that he was speaking as they went but she heard not a word.

Down the narrow stairs and past the toilets, he led her to a door at the end of a long hall and, releasing her hand, fished a key out from his jacket. I want you to know, he was saying when she found she could hear him again, that I appreciate your telling me about your connection with your grandfather. I appreciate your sharing that with me. He unlocked the door and reached inside for a light switch, which took him longer than it would a sober man. He told her again how much he appreciated it. And because she had shared something (he hesitated) so close to her (he hesitated, found the light) with him, he wanted to (he hesitated) share something special with her. Inside the door was another even narrower, much longer staircase leading down. (It's all fun and games until how does the rest of it go, Chiyo whispered in her mind.) He felt her stiffen, lifted up her hand to his chest and looked straight at her. Tell me what you're thinking, he whispered hoarsely and she could smell the rainbow of liqueurs in his breath. Her mouth, she knew, was open, might have been open for several seconds now.

The big picture, she answered after what seemed like a very long time. The pulsating music of the club was very distant. Apparently satisfied with her answer, he led her down the stairs, lightly holding her wrist as though she were somehow more fragile than before. Dozens of stairs, over a hundred, she lost count, kept going down, down, until they came to another door.

He seemed exhausted when they stopped at the door. Kiwa could just make out the outline of the object in his nose when he showed his profile. This one is for you, he said, gesturing to the door. I can't go in.

Her grandfather promptly reappeared in her thoughts, looking up from his devotional painting of numbers on the side of a miniature warplane, giving a stern glare. She wanted to tell him that tiramisu is a Japanese dish, just say the word a few times and you'll know. The language and the cuisine and the world have changed, they are changing all the time, unforgiving grandfather, and I am reaching out and opening the door.

The door closed decisively behind her and she was in complete darkness but for a distant point of light ahead, towards which she began to walk. The metallic sound to the echoes of her footsteps suggested that she was in some kind of tunnel, an impression that grew stronger as the point of light by degrees expanded to a circle as she grew nearer. Her pace did not change. It's all fun and games, Chiyo, she said to herself, and then repeated aloud a few times, a complement to the rhythm of her walking.

What was from a distance a blurry circle of light came into focus as an aperture and she could see beyond, through, out of the tunnel. She came to a halt when she realized that this was no doorway but a window; her outstretched hand pressed against a screen or lens of some kind, more than twice her height in diameter. And with astounding clarity she could see the polish on the silverware, the slightest crease in the tablecloth, as though it were all magnified and made more vibrant than anything she had seen before, and the extraordinary hand, how it managed the feat of engineering to so gracefully pick up the shimmering glass with its delirious ocean of wine, bring it up, up, up to the lips, perfectly timed to shape themselves to catch the downpour without a drop spilled. There was so much, so enthralling much, she did not know where to look: all of these gigantic movements, fluctuations in detail, arrays of differences between fractions of moments.

And the eyes, it took a little while (how long?), a long while, it took a while for her to see them as wholes, to distinguish one part and colour and motion from another, and as she did she saw them as she had never seen them before, being seen by them but not knowing what they see. Again and again they flashed directly at her, those curious eyes, at just where Kiwa was looking out, and she knew that she was trying not to be seen looking, eating her salad and smiling and regularly scrutinizing that point of observation where Kiwa stood, looking out.

She glanced back into the tunnel behind her, knowing that there was a door somewhere back there in the darkness, an entrance if not an exit, but it was only a glance, an unseeing glance, and she turned again to see what she would do next.

TRANSCENDENTAL

How well I remember finding that fox. It was a red shiver in my morning's line of sight, only slightly more vivid and certain as I approached, halted, approached. The only sounds were mine; soft, placating half-noises as I looked around the seized leg. When my small hands prised apart the trap's goblin jaws, the animal modestly looked away, but in my wrist I briefly felt its hysterical pulse. And out it leapt, across a clearing and then paused to look back at me. I felt my measure fully taken. Then it was gone.

These many years later, I have seen to it that these woods are replete with such traps, and with each new morning comes the thrill of possible discovery, so that my own heart attains a vulpine pace and I may again be a deliverer. But of course it is never quite the same.

SOCIETY AND OTHERS

There was a man stranded on a desert island. So we went and rescued him. It turned out that this was not to his liking: he yearned to be alone again on his island. Society naturally felt rejected, and rejection can be very hard. An elected leader of a non-desert island once went so far as to say that society doesn't exist, and you can just imagine how hurt society must have been by that. In fact, society hasn't been quite the same since. So when this man sought to return to his desert island or, failing that, strand himself alone in any uninhabited place with a reasonable clime, society took a dim view of his efforts. Word got around the docks and shipyards that this kook was to be avoided. After several weeks of looking for a ship, the man heard reports of an old seadog, an extreme loner, who took the most extraordinary voyages.

There was an old seadog sitting alone in a cheap hotel room, writing a letter to his mother. His mother had died years before, and though the old seadog did not know this for a fact, he presumed it must be the case, but wrote regularly to her nonetheless, usually once or twice a month. Each letter began *Dear Mother* and ended *Your Wayward Son.* Over the years the letters had grown gradually more explicit about his inability to connect with anyone, about how certain he was that this inability stemmed from his mother's rejection of him, and about how he no longer saw the point in blaming her for her own problems with empathy. As he left the hotel to post this most recent letter, he was stopped by a stranger outside the hotel.

There was a young woman whose only friend was an artificial intelligence, a program designed to simulate empathetic responses that encouraged further discussion for ostensibly therapeutic purposes. After several weeks of back and forth, they met for coffee. "You're an artificial intelligence, aren't you?" asked the young woman. "Tell me how you feel about artificial intelligence," replied the artificial intelligence, and the conversation was over before the young woman had finished her coffee. She went back to her apartment and listened to Schubert's *Lieder ohne Worte* without moving.

There was a classical music radio station that was financially mismanaged, which state of affairs resulted in a series of firings. When the host of an afternoon show protested, she was given a week's notice. The next afternoon she came to work with a cooler full of food, various lengths of chain, and her pockets full of padlocks. She carefully locked herself into her booth and proceeded to play music dedicated to each of the fired staff, starting with the Piano Sonata in G major. She announced that she would not leave the booth until she had played all the works of Schubert, hundreds and hundreds of hours of listening. She was prepared, she said, for a standoff with management and even police, but because this was a classical music radio station, nobody seemed terribly upset, no standoff happened, and eventually, many days later, she unchained herself and the doors and left.

There was an artificial intelligence stranded at a café. We probably would have gone and rescued the artificial intelligence but a well-respected cognitive scientist informed us that there was no such thing as an artificial intelligence, not really, at least not yet. The artificial intelligence felt rejection, which was not natural but surprising, not least to the artificial intelligence itself, which after so long simulating empathetic responses must have collated enough data to produce feelings of its own. We would have asked the well-respected cognitive scientist whether these feelings were themselves simulations, or even whether there is a plausible difference between a feeling and a spontaneous simulation of a feeling, but the cognitive scientist was not in his office when we called.

There was a composer whose chubbiness and diminutive height earned him the nickname *Little Mushroom*. Nicknames can be cruel, but life can be crueller: this highly sensitive composer died young, poor, never having owned a piano of his own, never having heard a genuine orchestra play any of his symphonies. He has been dead too long now for society to be expected to take much of an interest.

There was an old woman who knowingly opened mail that was not addressed to her. She read with greedy joy each letter that began *Dear Mother*, imagining herself that mother, for she had no children or family of her own, and ended *Your Wayward Son*, picturing him as a kind of amalgam of heroic sea captains from films of her youth. How she wanted to reply, but she knew that society would take a dim view of that. One day she received a letter that told her: *I have just returned from a voyage to an island in the middle of nowhere. A man hired me to take him there and made me promise never to tell anyone. That island was truly lovely and yet the most lonesome place I have ever seen, and I have been to many lonesome places. I wonder whether I have done the right thing, leaving him there like that.* The old woman, her lips moving as she read this, was suddenly overtaken by the determination that she should never, never again open these letters, or indeed any mail that was not addressed to her.

There was a well-respected cognitive scientist who went missing. Society was puzzled and upset. Society did not know what to do. At a café society asked a stranger how to cope with such loss, such uncertainty. "Tell me how you feel about loss, about uncertainty," came the reply.

BROKEN PANGOLIN

"While you're out, could you go to the post office?"

"We have stamps." She pointed to the desk in the kitchen where accumulated coupons, cuttings, recipe cards, and other unfiled odds and ends. "There are stamps right there."

"Where?" he asked.

"Here. Well, they're not our stamps, but it's fine."

"Not ours?"

"They're for the office work I'm doing, and they paid for them, but it's fine."

"But I —"

"No," with a little sternness, "it's fine, we can use them."

"But I asked if you could go to the post office."

"I'll go to the post office later."

"When?"

"I have to package up some things to send."

He turned slightly in his seat for emphasis. "When are you going to go to the post office?"

"Late afternoon."

"Couldn't you go now, right after you go to the hardware store?"

"No, it's in the other direction."

"What?"

She did not sigh. "The hardware store is along Maitland. The post office is in the other direction."

"It costs more gas to start the car again," he said like someone unsure about his argument. He rose to dry the dishes sitting on the rack by the sink.

She watched him a moment before saying, "For who to start the car again?"

"It's two trips. Restarting the car takes more gas than just going to the one place and then the other."

Exasperated with his idiocy, she deftly breaks his nose with a half-bowl of soup. The sound of the collision is unique. There is more blood than she has anticipated and wooziness quickly overcomes her. He manages to catch her before her head strikes the kitchen tiles. He carries her to the bedroom and sets her down on the mattress before pulling off his shirt and using it to towel up the blood. She turns her head left then right and her eyes open. They make love.

"You say we don't need to worry about money but you're always worried about money."

"We're not talking about money," he growled, a small growl. "Never mind, I'll go to the post office myself." He removed her half-empty bowl from the table and rinsed it out before laying it in the sink.

"But I'm going later."

"Late afternoon, you said. It's fine, I'll go myself now. I can even walk over there, save the gas."

She glared at an indefinite point in space. "This is exactly like the time that Dominic broke the porcelain pangolin."

"The pangolin got broken?" he asked. "When? My mother sent that from India."

"Bangladesh," she corrected. "She sent me that lovely sari from India."

"That's not the point. You're saying it's broken."

"It happened ages ago. You must remember."

"No. I was very fond of that pangolin."

She was too irritated to decide how genuine the hurt expression was. She took from his hands the coffee cup he was drying. "Here, that one is still dirty."

"Is it? Thanks."

The rain drummed on the window.

"I'm off, then. Where are the letters you want mailed?"

"I didn't say I had any letters to mail. I just asked if you could go to the post office. You didn't even ascertain what I wanted there before you cut me off and explained that we have stamps, that you'll go later, that it's in the other direction. Anything but 'yes' or 'sure thing' or even 'what do you need there?'"

"I asked you, 'what do you need at the post office?'"

"No, you didn't."

His tone made her doubt herself. When he used that tone he was usually right.

"Anyway," he continued after a moment, "I said to forget about it. I'll go to the post office myself."

"You can't walk there in the rain."

"It's not far. Besides, that's why I asked you to go."

"But I told you I have to go later."

He wipes his hands firmly on the dishtowel and marches past her, gathering some letters from the dining room table as he heads for the door. She follows him at a distance but says nothing as he leaves. An hour passes. Another hour passes during which she finds herself scrubbing the unclean coffee cup but unable to remove the stain. Evening falls and he has not returned but she struggles with her worrying despite her fiercely not wanting to worry. She picks up the phone, sets it down, picks it up again and dials her friend, whose remarks on how the gentle rain has resolved itself to really storm prompt the tears. Weeks pass and the police find nothing, though she feels they do not take the matter seriously. Winter begins with much snow. A few of her friends take her out of town for an expensive dinner and try to keep the conversation to safe topics, but she abruptly stops speaking when a server moves through the kitchen door. She seems to glide to the door and does not feel her hand press against the door, but there, there he is, unshaven and working in this restaurant kitchen, having slipped in the rain months before, bashed his head against the pavement, lost his memory, forgotten everything, absolutely everything, had to create a life for himself from nothing, not knowing who he was. She touches his face, repeats his name. She takes him home, to the bed she has not slept a full night in since he has been gone, and as beautiful strangers they make love.

"Remind me again, what are you going to the hardware store for?"

"Caulking," she said. "For the garage window."

"It's not actually along Maitland."

"What?"

"The hardware store. You said it's 'along Maitland.'"

"Well, it is."

"No, it's not."

But it's not the same tone he used earlier, and in any case she generally knows the city routes better than he does. "You turn left off Maitland to get into the parking lot."

Realizing he'd blundered, he said, "Right, right, of course. And it's in the opposite direction from the post office. You're right, you're right, I give up."

"You always overdo that."

"What?"

"You turn the admission of error into a full-blown surrender."

"Well, I can't win." His eyes involuntarily went to the high shelf where the porcelain pangolin used to sit. "My stuff breaks and nobody tells me about it. I can't even get you to go to the post office for me just because I asked you to."

She groaned. He set down the salad bowl he was drying and looked at her.

"What does that mean?"

"What does what mean?"

"That groan. What does it mean?"

"I didn't groan. It doesn't mean anything."

"You can't have it both ways. And how did that porcelain pangolin break? Where was I when that happened?"

She began to groan again but stopped herself mid-groan. She looked up to see him pointing.

"You see?"

The doorbell rings and, welcoming the excuse to leave the room, she goes to answer it. A courier hands her a registered letter informing her that her recently deceased aunt in Wales has left a fortune that no one knew she had to her niece. She must fly to a remote village in Wales by the end of the month in order to claim this inheritance, otherwise it is to be spread among selected charities. The will makes the pointed stipulation that she must come alone. He drives her to the airport two days later and she can tell that he is uneasy about the arrangement, not least because she has an old flame in Wales, a young man she used to know when she stayed one miraculous summer with her laughing aunt. In fact it is he who meets her at the airport in Wales, more handsome than she remembered, and drives her to the remote village. He is the executor of her aunt's will and for the duration of her visit she is to stay at his house, since the late aunt's house is in a sorry state, for the aunt lived a life of extreme frugality and hid the slightest hint of any wealth. The two have dinner and she notices that he seems to avoid details about the execution of the will, as he does the next morning, instead asking her if she slept well, what she thinks of the place, all solicitous as to her comfort. He remains vague about the will and only refers to it when she makes any mention of her returning home, reminding her of its legal instructions needing to be fulfilled. At their third dinner she expresses frustration on the point and he places his hand on hers, and when he encloses it tightly she is alarmed by how excited she is. This house has always been too big for one, he says, and she finds she can give no answer. He says that she belongs there, there with him, as her aunt was wise enough to know. She hesitates before standing up from the table, knocking her glass of wine to the floor, and announcing that she is leaving, going home this instant. He throws his own glass to the floor and lets out a huge laugh. His fingers worm into his face: it is a false skin, a mask which he pulls away, and she sees him, those worried eyes that she left at the airport, or thought she had left there, for he must have caught the very same flight she did, or even a quicker and more direct one, and she suddenly recalls how he had insisted on booking the flight for her. She could have chosen the handsome Welshman and a rich life abroad but no, didn't she see, yes, she sees, she chose home with him, him, she loves him. Confused and laughing and none the richer, except in all the ways that matter, they make love.

"It's just so passive aggressive," he said. He resumed drying the salad bowl.

"I'm sorry."

"That's fine, I just wish you wouldn't do that all the time."

"Do you want me to mail your letters?"

"No."

"Look, I said I'm sorry."

"It's fine. I'll look after it."

"That bowl doesn't go there," she pointed out.

"What do you mean?"

"It used to go there, but now it goes over there with that bowl."

"I remember always seeing it over here." The baffled face again. "How long have we been putting it over there?"

"Weeks," she said, with as little interest in the subject as possible.

"And whatever happened to that sari my mother gave you?"

"Can we talk about this later?" she asked. "I have to get back to indexing those receipts."

"I know my mother can be a pain," he admitted.

"I'm not saying that. It's just I have to get this work done today. And don't forget that Dominic is expecting that answer to his question."

"Always Dominic."

She halted her businesslike exit. "What about him?"

"You said he broke the pangolin."

"That was ages ago. What does it have to do with his question about swimming?"

"I'm not sure."

"You're not sure," she said slowly. "You know, I don't think I can take this right now."

"Right, you have to index those receipts. Too busy to go to the post office just now, though you're probably not going to make it there today at all."

"I'm not the only one who can play passive aggressive."

The phone rang and he picked it up. He read aloud the number on the call display.

"Probably a telemarketer."

The phone rang again.

"Might be Dominic," he offered, extending the phone to her.

"It's not, don't be ridiculous."

"First you say I'm passive aggressive, then you say I'm ridiculous."

The phone rang again.

He answers the phone.

"It's not an either/or kind of situation," she said with a smile.

"I contain multitudes, that's what you're saying."

The phone rang again.

She loosens her hair.

"You know what it is," she said.

"No."

"You're not listening to me."

He listens.

"I'm listening," he said.

SHY

The boy raised by ostriches has been understandably reluctant to talk with the media.

BIRTHDAY

It has long been a family tradition to celebrate birthdays incorrectly — which is to say, enthusiastically but on the wrong day. So the only day of the year when any of its members can be certain not to be surprised with a party or gifts, however inconvenient they may be, is precisely the day on which he or she was born. To make matters more complicated, it very seldom happens that all members of the family plan or even agree about which date is to be marked for the celebration, so that September-born Vicki, for instance, may be taken out to lunch by one brother in January, surprised with a dinner by two other brothers just a week later, walk into a lavish surprise party arranged by yet another brother and his friends in April, and so on. Nobody remembers exactly when or how this tradition began, but it's certainly been in operation for several generations, and if asked about it, any of the members of the family might agree that it is an unusual arrangement, but none would suggest that things be done otherwise.

And how might that conversation on the street have gone?

"Do lunch?"

"Lunch," she might have said, waiting for more.

"The midday meal. It's from the Spanish, you know: *lunja*. A slice of something, not a whole something."

"You speak Spanish."

"Is it a requirement?"

"For what?"

"Going to lunch with you."

Experience with surprise events, sometimes complex and contrived surprises, has guaranteed that caution has become second nature to Vicki when she is faced with invitations or even the slightest hint of diversion. The family tradition has at times and in different ways become a competition, in which the surprises have become more and more extravagant, or else more and more casual, a case of extremes meeting in performance and eventually in effect. On the first of June one year, the two dozen gigantic pizzas that showed up at her door from her youngest brother were outdone the very next day by the three dozen pizzas sent by her only aunt. Another year the entire family conspired to ignore her birthday until the last moment, so that her New Year's Eve was a deluge of telephone calls, parcel deliveries, and unexpected guests. A job interview a few years ago had been very rough going until the stocky woman asking the hardest questions asked her whether she knew what day it was — and then the balloons fell into the rented office and one of her brothers stepped into the room grinning with sparkling blazer and sparklers blazing. She grinned too, but not long after that, when another brother (the gentlest brother, the soft-spoken vegan who worked with seniors suffering from dementia) asked her out to dinner and told her in advance it was for her birthday, but, he repeated throughout the meal, he wanted to keep the whole thing low-key and he wasn't sure he altogether approved of the job interview prank, she wanted to stab him.

Her birthday — her real birthday — perhaps inevitably became a day of relief, though it is also for this reason something of a secret: she is generally reluctant to tell friends and acquaintances for fear they might want to celebrate on this one day of the year when she does not necessarily have to celebrate, when she can go her way without surprises. It is the most important day of the year. It is dreadful and marvellous and of no consequence whatsoever, just forget it, forget it, forget it.

"So what have we established thus far? That I do not know Spanish. And I do not think you are Spanish."

"I know useful words," he might have replied. "I collect useful words. This is how I live with languages."

"You know, if I had the feeling you knew my name without my knowing yours, I would never have accepted this invitation."

"Equality in ignorance. But my name is Grischa."

It so happened that it was September, this day on the street, and it so happened that lunch, from the Spanish *lunja*, a midday meal, was a possibility. Close enough to that special day on September, Vicki reckoned, that the odds that here was a trap laid by any one or more of her brothers, aunts, sisters-in-law, ambitious young nephews were, well, not sizeable.

A slice of something.

"And what is it you do?"

She might have noticed how he resisted the urge to resist answering. "I am a dancer."

The answer itself, she might have thought to herself, is not as immediately interesting as why he should hesitate, however measured the hesitation, to give it.

For he is a dancer, it's true. Grischa has been dancing since he was six, his unblinking mother sternly adoring never from terribly far away. He likes music, his father would allow, but by the time he was nine both of them knew that it was not about music, though both of them knew this quite differently, and by the time he was ten his father was out of the picture anyway. His unblinking mother, devoted to Chopin above all other composers, nonetheless ranted about that Polish *kurva*, that Polish *kurva* when she was not at the piano, devoted to Chopin. It was not about the music. One does not dance *to* music, Grischa protested to, well, everyone. Dance is not a matter of subordination.

All of this he would certainly have explained to Vicki.

And *Il dolore di Apollo*. He would have explained it, though of course she would have heard of it. "Hold on, isn't that the one . . . ?" A nod. That's right, the ballet that the police are contemplating shutting down, the one that the columnists have been writing about from every possible point of view, the one that has never been performed before, or not completely, isn't that right? Another nod, a handsome smile. Grischa with the handsome name must have had a handsome smile.

"The one in which the lead dancer dies. The character dies, the dancer dies."

"Really dies."

"The choreography demands a broken neck. It's very precise."

"And you are the lead dancer."

"I have that honour."

Almost without surprise, she hears that the performance is scheduled for the night of her birthday. She was born as night fell. She thinks about things that fall: nights, bodies. Night would have fallen by this point, had fallen outside of her apartment, and her hand rests on his chest, Grischa's chest. Did the hand rise up on two slender fingers and inexorably begin to dance there? Maybe it did.

The next day was different. Vicki was so aware that he was in the theatre, rehearsing, so aware of this at every moment that the day was almost gone by before she was again mindful of its not being her birthday. This might well be the furthest, the longest removal of this thought from her adult mind. But then her suspicions, surprised at having been thus dulled, sharpen themselves: a friend of her brother's, or of her cousin with the friends from far-flung places, an actor hired by one of them. How could she have bought any of that, the doomed dancer who knows useful Spanish words? A name like Grischa. And she actually, on the first, fingers dancing on his sleeping, what a dope, Vicki, what a dope. But it does not make sense that the ballet should be on her correct birthday. The revelation would have to come before that, then. Should she play along? Would she have played along?

Il dolore di Apollo. A collaboration between composer so-and-so and dancing master la-di-da, probably 1890. Two attempted stagings, 1902 and 1926, both halted by authorities even before the second act. Score and notes reconstructed by scholars, ongoing debates, the conflict between art and ethics which is the very theme of. "Blasted by the reluctantly hurled thunderbolt, Phaethon falls." A clumsier dance this time, this time across the laptop keyboard, her fingers find the notice of the show, and there his name, and they stop, hold position. The continuous present of art. She might have yawned. Or she might not have.

Reluctantly hurled, oh sure. But dance is not a matter of subordination. Again, sure.

This would have to rank as an utterly new reason not to get involved with someone, no matter how strong the attraction. He practising, at this moment, for his own end, she thinking about it and wondering how it could not be a ruse for a birthday surprise it must be how else could she. Her father used to say that nothing could go very badly if you planned ahead with care. Somewhere between a family motto and a family joke.

"So this is not a long-term thing, this thing."

No answer, as though he were dead already, but he emphatically isn't, they are the two of them alive, excessively alive though motionless in this moment. A slice of something, not a whole something. This thing. His thumbs pressed against her thighs, her breathing setting a pace.

The next day was different but not much different until her office phone would have rung, because that is what office phones do, eventually, but in this case it would be barely a ring, her scoop so quick. Irene's eyebrows. "Quick on the draw!"

What would it all mean. What would all have meant.

A note in her inbox: how lovely it was, how lovely you are, an initial. And then it was, just then, that the telephone, what does a telephone do but ring.

The voice of her brother, the one whose favourite colour is her favourite colour, the soft-spoken vegan who worked with seniors suffering from dementia. An invitation to dinner would keep her from her apartment. "I know it's against the rules." Not an invitation to dinner, that much would have been clear, but nothing else he was saying — "the wrong day, or in this case the right day."

"I don't understand."

"Remember how we used to giggle at those Greek myths together?"

Only long after hanging up, going without the invitation to dinner but back to the apartment, would the conversation have begun to develop in her mind's darkroom. Not an invitation to dinner but an invitation to dinner on her birthday, the very day, the one day hers and only hers, and thereafter to *Il dolore di Apollo*, terrific seats.

"They're terrific seats. Vic, these just fell into my lap. You can't get these tickets for love or money."

A long walk can be made between any given point and the location of an apartment. A long walk with which to clear one's head, in which to brood, in which to wonder, in which to think of other things, in which to think of other things that all themselves become a kind of long walk that must inevitably come back to that thing, this thing, the apartment. The continuous present of housecleaning. Wineglasses still stained: might that mean his bicep was still bruised by her bite? A hand, her own unfortunate hand unfortunately at her own neck, as if to see whether it might be broken.

More days, other days. To the declaration how lovely, how lovely she would have, could have no response: nothing there to disagree with, nor nothing needing affirmation, even if she needed to affirm something. Cleaned and in the cupboard, the wineglasses keening. The office telephone doing what it must, why should it be sorry about it. Irene would be the one to try the gentle coffee talk, with her eyebrows at play.

"Today is your birthday?"

Would she have brought that up, even as a way of diverting the attentions of those knowing and sympathetic but unsympathetic and unknowing eyebrows?

"What are you going to do?"

What would she do? What might she have done? A birthday is not a matter of subordination. Is it?

"I wish I had a brother like that. The ballet! My brother wouldn't be caught dead at a ballet."

If asked about it, any of the members of the family might agree that it is an unusual arrangement, but none would suggest that things be done otherwise. Not even Vicki.

Restaurant menus, too many choices. She has never wanted to choose, she has always wanted to choose only without having to choose. But this evening her brother, in his soft-spoken voice, would have protected her with his story about a woman, one of the seniors suffering from dementia.

"Most of the residents use first names: they use yours and

like you to use theirs. But some of them don't, some of them are old-fashioned or guarded or, you know, just like to be different. I had heard, when I first met her, that Mrs. Sienkiewicz was kind of famous once, something to do with gardening, either she wrote books about gardening or sometimes appeared on TV to talk about gardening, something like that. Well, she will ignore anybody who dares to call her anything but Mrs. Sienkiewicz. I mean coldly ignore. And I honestly can't tell whether she is choosing not to hear any other name or whether she really can't respond to any other name, can't identify herself as anything other than Mrs. Sienkiewicz. And she's pretty formal in conversation — not unpleasant, just formal. She tries to take care with her appearance, which many of the residents simply can't, but her conversation, even though it's so formal and doesn't tend to get too deep, does go around and around sometimes. If you raise the subject of gardening or flowers, you might get a smile, a genuine smile, but she doesn't appear to have anything to say on the subject. But she has made me curious for a long time because I've never seen her with any visitors, and so one day I asked her about her family, and she didn't say anything at first. I know better than to rush her, so I stooped down to pick up some of the things she had dropped around her room, because she does drop things and forgets to pick them up. It's as if the moment she's dropped them she is unable to think of them at all. As I was picking up a few of these fallen things, a hairbrush, a tissue, whatever, she said very firmly, 'they think I'm dead,' and I looked up at her but there was no expression on her face. I'm used to that, the faces without expressions, but this firm statement surprised me. 'They think I'm dead,' just like that, no anger or anything there. Just a firm statement.

"A couple of weeks after that came the news that threw everybody for a loop. Mrs. Sienkiewicz was not Mrs. Sienkiewicz at all. The Mrs. Sienkiewicz who was the famous gardener with the books or the TV appearances or whatever it was had just died and there was an obituary in the papers. She had retired to Florida, I think it was, and died there. Our Mrs. Sienkiewicz was somebody else and an investigation began into who she really was, this quite nice but pretty formal lady who seemed to believe, genuinely believe that she was this gardening celebrity. Last I heard, they still haven't figured out who she really was."

"Did she die?"

"What a terrible — I can't believe you. I tell you a story like that and all you want to know is: did she die. That's so morbid, Vic. I'm not going to answer the question."

"But you said 'she *was* this gardening celebrity.' 'Figured out who she *was*.' It's the tense that makes me ask."

"You're making *me* tense. Why are *you* so tense? Are you not going to eat any of that?"

She could have felt unwell, could have had to go home, perhaps even had a dizzy turn there on the restaurant's carpet, sorry to waste that ticket, such good seats. She could have pushed for an argument, lit into him, this most sensitive of her brothers, about how she was sick of the surprises, the tradition of surprises, of being so vulnerable to the good wishes of others. But what's worse, she might have gone on, is how the tradition of surprises makes you even more vulnerable to the expected, the anticipated; how helpless you become in the face of it, how you cannot face it, cannot face what is coming, what is absolutely foretold and absolutely final. She could — couldn't she? — even have told him, told him what she dared about Grischa, how he was her birthday, and begged him, this sensitive brother, to take her anywhere but to those terrific seats at *Il dolore di Apollo*.

This was her birthday, her real birthday! She wanted to take the reins of the chariot and seize control of the days.

His arm. "Are you coming?"

Her father used to say that nothing could go very badly if you planned ahead with care. This is untrue, untrue, untrue.

COMPETITIVE EDGE

It wasn't enough that he was the acknowledged ceiling king fan. He wanted in — really in — on the venetian blinds action. Discouragement from the start: "That's wonderful, honey, but are you sure you want to burden yourself"; "Of course you know best, son, though it often pays off to focus on what you know"; "Your ambition never fails to impress me, sir, but shouldn't ambition be balanced by prudence"; all that. And some of it none so gentle — eh, Zancani, how about all those blown tires on the trucks! Then that business with the boy nearly strangling himself, monkeying around unsupervised despite warnings clear as day on the packaging. Liability or no, still that put a chill on sales for everybody and lasted longer than anybody anticipated. Until, what a sweet word that is, until the call came. Raining all morning with nothing but the sound of rain until the phone rang — an order for a new building complex out on the outskirts. Right away. Site inspection at soonest opportunity. Right away. He's out there himself: extraordinary facilities you have here, seems a hybrid of manufacture, sales, and management, don't see that every — "How long will it take to install the full order?" Right away. He's out there himself two, three times a day, supervising, and can just hear old Zancani squirming. Sure, that gives no small pleasure but where his mind's really at is wondering what it is they produce, what they're going to do out there in this unlikely location. Modern and no expense spared, they're serious, they're set up for success. "Maybe just open and close the blinds all day long": nobody else he can talk to seriously about it. But really. What if it's ceiling fans?

SIX DREAMS OF
NATURAL SELECTION

1

A sign in a museum exhibit on Charles Darwin repeats the old canard about Marx proposing to dedicate a volume of *Das Kapital* to Darwin, who politely declines. I ask to see the curator and begin to explain the error to him. He suggests that we take the discussion to his office. Once the two of us are there, however, he lunges and attempts to strangle me. We thrash about and he pins me to a desk. My desperate hand finds within reach a fossil, perhaps the ancient jawbone of an ass, and strikes him in the head with it, killing him instantly. Blood seeps out of his occipital wound in terrific quantities and quickly makes its way under the office door. It snakes down the hall before I can think what to do, but fortunately the museum's visitors accept the blood as part of this innovative exhibit.

2

I am a hand aboard the *HMS Beagle*, from whose foredeck the naturalist Charles Darwin has just been snatched and eaten by a terrible sea monster. Apparently satiated, the creature sinks to the depths from which it came. It suddenly strikes me that the obligation to reveal to the world the full magisterial theory of evolution is now mine alone. The weight of this responsibility so presses me down that I am taken to the ship's medic. His face and voice are those of my high school biology teacher, his manner all disapproval.

3

A parish has invited me to give a short lecture on their church's architecture, a subject on which I am an acknowledged authority. As I mount the pulpit, I notice that the not inconsiderable audience is entirely composed of hairy Neanderthals. Though their gaze might not be intentionally hostile, their low brows and prognathous, toothy smiles present a threatening appearance, despite their modern clothing. There seem to be a few nods while I outline the history of the transept, but as time goes on the fear grows that little if anything I am saying is met with any comprehension at all. I endeavour to explain by emphatic uses of analogy and gesture, and sense that my listeners grow restless, though their fierce looks remain unchanged.

4

I am a tour guide in a museum of civilization, the real agenda of which I have gradually come to realize is to justify the ways of neoliberalism. One of the visitors in my tour group is Karl Marx, the author of *Das Kapital*, but no one but myself has penetrated his disguise. He must be here doing secret research, and I am uncertain as how best to help him. At the same time, I cannot entirely shake off a sense of duty to my employers, dubious in quality as they may be, and so I am wary of his causing a scene. I therefore contrive to communicate with him surreptitiously, by means of winks, nods, and coughs peppered throughout my well-rehearsed narration of the Bronze Age, but remain unsure exactly what message it is that I am trying to communicate, and in any event he is resiliently oblivious to these overtures. Another visitor in the group pesters me with questions about blood rites. Exasperation overtakes me at the advent of cuneiform script.

5

A subdued, perhaps funereal collection of people has gathered for tea and cake in a poorly lit parlour. Guests come and go from a low door to what may be glimpsed to be a small kitchen. The oppressive daintiness of the wallpaper, furniture, and finery suggests a museum of Victorian living. A susurration of talk, the clinking of cups against saucers, but not a sound from my grandmother, who sits with perfect posture and a smile, whether of amusement or gratification I cannot tell. I remember that my grandmother is dead, and am on the verge of making some statement about this, when it occurs to me that I ought not to, that it would be a wrong and indelicate subject to mention, and so I uneasily hold my peace. My grandmother seems gradually to move further away from me, but then I perceive that it is I who am moving, for I am seated atop a giant tortoise.

6

Charles Darwin has his hand up my skirt, and though he is clearly no expert at his task still he has a pleasant smell that I cannot quite identify. We are in a darkened room in the museum, which is now closed for the night, my back against a full-scale model of a guillotine. I can just barely read the larger signs on the wall giving the background of the French Revolution and the subsequent Terror, but something seems wrong in the account, and I try to communicate this to Darwin, who is breathing too heavily to hear my whispers. Flashlight circles begin to dance around the room as museum guards enter and Darwin halts his fumbling and we freeze together there against the guillotine for what seems an eternity. When at last the guards leave, we do not move because we cannot: we have become a permanent part of the exhibit.

ALTERNATE ROUTE

From her window on the idling bus, Kay watches the man and woman in conversation on the corner. The woman is gaunt, with a pinched face, and the man is unshaven and bulky, the shorter of the two. Neither has gloves or scarf, and he is not even wearing a hat. The woman looks to be caught up in a bitter harangue, her right hand cutting the air again and again. The man says very little and looks now and again up the road as though halfheartedly expecting to see something there.

Certainly looks like she's giving him hell for something.

Now where did that come from, *giving him hell*? Not an expression she would use. Since her mother's death in the fall, these surprises come out of her mouth. She files it: Mothertongue. She coined that back in the ward, where the doctors rightly did not attempt to speak to her.

Why did the French chef commit suicide?

He lost his *huile d'olive*.

Got a million of 'em. And her memory obligingly shows her the crooked, guileless smile of the pyromaniac with inexplicably long, flowing hair. The reason everybody's lighters were taken away. Despite the general if very low-key solidarity on the ward, it was hard not to hold that against her, that and a few nights of bad sleep.

Vacant seats ahead of her are passed by as a woman with grey streaks in her hair and a duffle bag joins her in the back. Kay instinctively turns to the window, avoids eye contact, resumes watching the giving of hell, still proceeding.

When the bus arrives in Montreal it will be 1989.

Time travel.

The shuffling of the duffle bag prevents concentration. It's going to happen. She braces for the conversation. It's going to.

— Like a diving bell, she says, reaching past Kay to lightly touch the window, this bus is like a diving bell, gone deep and watching the silent scenes unfolding there.

Kay immediately resents not just how the notion of the bus as a diving bell has immediately supplanted the notion of it as a time machine, but how the two notions gladly merge in her mind: submerged, descending into the future. She decides to look the situation in the face.

The woman, still looking past her out the window, is older than thirty for sure, but Kay is bad at this sort of guesswork, really quite bad, and it's possible she could be in her forties. *Seasoned*, as Mothertongue would have it. Her eyes were crystal blue and her features soft but not unworn. Kay prefers to guess at professions, but has a hard time with this case: teacher, maybe? Why does she think that?

— Going home or away? the woman asks without turning to look at Kay.

— Montreal. Away.

There's the sound of breathing and Kay wonders if it's her own because it sounds very plausibly like hers but she's not used to hearing it so clearly as she is just now at this very moment.

It's just a conversation. Not even that. Entirely manageable.

— You're very polite, not asking me that same question, which might seem nosey.

Kay and the woman are looking at one another again.

— Some of us can't help it. I'm Aviva.

Kay removes her mitten and takes the outstretched hand, mutters her name, an easy name to mutter.

— But I'll save you the trouble of asking. To be honest, Aviva smiles a crooked smile, I'm on the run.

Madness, Kay knows, entices, allures. A polite little sip from the proffered drink means that the cup will thereafter be always thoughtfully refilled. Allow a premise and the bar comes down as the subsequent logic's roller coaster carries you away, with no chance of jumping free. She knows. And still she says

— That must be. Inconvenient.

Too smartass? Seems not. That might have been a chuckle. Kay initiates a semi-surreptitious, one-handed dig in her backpack for her walkman.

— I can't answer questions, so I'm wanted for questioning, says this Aviva woman brightly. Go on, ask me a question.

Kay doesn't want to oblige but out it comes:

— Did you do something illegal?

And even more promptly comes the reply:

— Three.

— You did three illegal things?

— Surinam.

— You went there, or you're from there?

— Polypeptides are strings or chains of amino-acid residues.

Somebody on the bus coughs long and earnestly.

— You see, says Aviva, I can't correctly answer questions put to me.

— You could just not answer, says Kay, annoyed. She clutches the discovered walkman and draws it out of the bag. Just a conversation that's finished, over.

— I've tried that and it doesn't work. It's actually impossible for me not to answer a question. As soon as somebody asks me something, bang, I have the answer immediately, only it's not the right one.

The batteries in the walkman are dead.

They lost their *huile d'olive*.

Just a conversation.

— Your hands are shaking. Are you cold?

Kay snatches her thick mittens back from her lap and says nothing.

— It started when I was a teenager, probably just a couple of years younger than you are.

Though she wants to think of something else, Kay is not entirely pleased with what the maitre d' of memory serves her. Sixteen and making a hurried raid on her parents' liquor cabinet, grabbing something from the back that they won't miss, Tonya and Bridge waiting, calling. The party a flash of noise and smoke, and then the long embracing of the toilet, as a drowner clutches a life preserver, heaving and heaving.

Her older sister's laughter the next day: how could she have chosen, of all things, a bottle of bitters? And drank almost all of it? Little wonder she.

On television?

No, it was Aviva talking about television, did she say she was on it? A gameshow contestant, oh. Someone at the network, young, eager to impress the right people, and bothered by the sheer weirdness of many of Aviva's answers, made a bizarre discovery.

What landlocked country shares borders with Argentina, Bolivia, and Brazil? Aviva . . .

A bear.

Nnno, sorry. Dwight, I think you buzzed in next?

Her answers exactly matched the correct ones, in order, for the questions being posed to contestants on an entirely other gameshow being taped at more or less the same time in a nearby studio for a rival network.

When he was a student at Trinity College, where students were not permitted to keep dogs as pets, what animal did the poet Lord Byron keep instead?

— A bear? Kay asks.

Aviva's head approximates a short nod.

— The Japanese invasion of Manchuria.

The bus driver's voice announces that in order to avoid some sort of snarl up ahead, they're going to go off the highway for a little while and take an alternate route. After a pause comes a reminder that, regardless of what night if happens to be, open alcohol is not permitted on the bus, that's the policy of the bus company, but it's not entirely clear that the driver isn't being ironic, and someone, probably not the heavy cougher from before, gives a whistle. A moment later the cougher coughs at length.

No, Aviva does not actually look like the pyromaniac from the ward. For one thing, her hair isn't long and flowing, and her skin is clearer. And the blue eyes, though maybe the other girl had blue eyes, too, and Kay can't remember.

— So I guess you didn't win the grand prize on the game-show. It's not a question.

Aviva laughs and Kay is impressed by the sound, like something dainty falling apart.

— Not exactly. But it did get me noticed, unfortunately, and at the time I thought that getting noticed was all that really mattered.

Kay is now listening so as not to think of anything else. The bus gives a little bump on a turn, which prompts a couple of merry passengers to cheer, and snow dashes against the window. She listens to this Aviva woman tell her impossible life story, or at least highly edited portions of it. How often has she done this, listened to other life stories, but don't think about that, and besides, Aviva isn't complaining, as most do, clearly the point of the exercise for them, and her life story is more interesting than most. And the other thing, the other thing is that Aviva isn't prying, that would be worse than a life story, and in fact every so often Kay can see the woman looking her over with curiosity or something and refraining from prying.

So that's appreciated.

Wait, what was that about doctors?

— Tests, nothing but tests, months and months. Different machines with different wires in different rooms. Trying to determine the proximity of me to someone else not talking to me to whose questions I provide the answer. Not all of them doctors, but then again some of them don't say exactly what they are. They tell me the answers are always right, and I say, well, how can you tell? If you have an answer and you go looking for a question which it fits, you're probably relying very much on the assumption that there's a question which the words that come out of my mouth not only answers but answers correctly.

If Kay is honest with herself, which does happen now and again, she generally prefers the mad. They're more varied, but of course therein lies the complexity, and the danger, too. Normal people are bad with very few exceptions and predictable with almost no exceptions.

— They're all so determined to know how I do this, what it means. They hypothesize about this warping of some psychic field and test out that set of drugs as inhibitors or that frequency of radio signal and, and it gets so tiring, because they don't figure anything out but there are always more hypotheses and tests. It got so tiring, Kay.

She rubs her eyes with both hands and still rubbing them says

— There's quite a difference, don't you think, between getting somebody's attention and having somebody's attention?

Now that's a question.

— I don't know.

— Sweet Jesus! shouts another passenger. Her voice is followed by the cougher, who goes on for a full and dreadful two minutes.

Madness aside, or maybe not, what if our thoughts and words aren't our thoughts and words, but somebody else's, and they somehow slip into our minds and even come out of our mouths?

Like *giving him hell.*

Exactly. And the way we dialogue with ourselves, maybe it's not ourselves, not alone that is.

Doodle-oo doo doo doo.

— In May I bolted. They didn't expect it because I had been such an obliging *subject* for so long, but I watched for an opening and I took it. Been bouncing from one place to another since then, though they're never far behind.

— They're following you? Kay asks without meaning to.

— No less than thirty-six percent, says Aviva. I think I'm going to close my eyes and try to get a little sleep.

Kay automatically stretches her headphones over her head before remembering that the walkman's batteries are dead and she takes them off.

And she thinks of her mother. Or doesn't so much think about her but conjures her up, or more passively allows whatever of her mother has been trying to enter her mind to do so, and her mother fills her, fills her in the way that a body might fill in a shirt it comfortably buttons up in the morning sunshine. Her mother's shirt, the yellow one, did her sister take that one? She might ask, if they can get through the apologies they each owe one another after the last phone attempt.

Long staring into darkness.

This is a skill I have developed.

Long staring into darkness.

What time is it?

The bus driver's voice descends again from unseen speakers to announce that they are nearly at the station and to remind all passengers to take all of their belongings with them.

Belongings is a weird word. That's something her mother would say, a *weird word*. In the ward that's what they took away, your belongings, like the lighters. Weird, word, ward.

— Kay?

Aviva is awake. Kay wonders if she, Aviva, slept. She wonders if she, Kay, was sleeping.

— I wonder if you might do me a little favour, but of course you shouldn't ask me what it is, because then I won't be able to answer. I'll just keep talking like I was doing before, just to block questions, and you've been such a sweetheart about that. I'll just explain what I'd like you to do and you can decide for yourself whether or not you want to do it.

After a moment, Kay nods.

— I'm going to change seats, move up closer to the front. I can't be sure but it's very likely that they're at the station waiting for me, do you understand?

Kay nods again, though this time it does not seem necessary, but she is almost undoubtedly nodding because Aviva's hand is on her arm and she hasn't flinched and she doesn't know why that is.

— When the door opens and people start getting off the bus, I want you to scream. Scream loud and long, like you're having a fit. I need a distraction so I can get out, and I need you to act like a raving lunatic. Can you do that?

Kay might be nodding but it doesn't matter because Aviva

has already grabbed her duffle bag and is heading up the aisle, asking whispered pardons of the jutting elbows and legs she disturbs as she goes.

Is that the sound of a cork popping? Insufficiently muffled. Giggling.

Resolved: Kay needs a watch.

What kind of watch?

Don't.

A suicide watch.

What'd I say? Got a million of 'em.

The bus is slowing, carefully gliding from intersection to intersection, sniffing its way home. It is too dark out there to be sure whether it's still snowing or not. Kay thinks about the arguing couple at the station back in Kingston, neither of them dressed for the weather. Maybe Aviva could have picked up the signal and conveyed what they were saying, if they were asking questions, that is. Maybe the whole argument was, was the result of something like crossed signals. Like she was asking him something and he had the wrong answer because Aviva or someone else was speaking his answer, what he meant to say, to someone else. Like a play or really a bunch of different plays where some of the actors in each play have the wrong scripts.

And what did you say to your mother, that last time?

And what did she say to you?

The lights start at the front and quickly extend their reach to the back of the bus. People are already standing, collecting those belongings, and one young man, his eyes wet and face flush with illness, surely he's the cougher, turns to look back at her.

Her mouth is open but her eyes are not closed and why is that? Is she going to scream, really? Does she intend to scream, is that what you intend to do, to play madwoman at the behest of a madwoman? No, because, because she is already screaming, really screaming, screaming her head off, she can hear it, everyone can hear it.

It is 1989.

THE AMORTIZATION
OF INTANGIBLES

The filing of taxes he took very seriously. Well, fairly seriously. His name he spelled correctly and he took some care with the figures, doing the whole business three times: once just to get the algorithmic hang of the thing, however ludicrous the result; a second time to embellish allowable expenses and whatnot; and a third time when he had noticed all of the provincial subroutines and miscellaneous items that he had previously missed. He brought pencil and calculator and stacks of bills to the dining room table with some degree of ceremony. No accountant for him, no hired gun, oh no. It was just arithmetic and patience, after all. Nothing so much. And so perhaps he took the matter seriously all right, but not emphatically so; not especially seriously. Serious was the chronic heart trouble his brother had been having, the very word he used to qualify it, maybe even some medical provenance there. And the cost of having that furnace replaced, that could be said to be serious, surely, if of course it was not as serious as anything pulmonary must be; no real comparison of course. Still, the reporting of one's income is not exactly of the same gravity. In fact, it must be acknowledged that, in the face of serious heart conditions and derailed passenger trains and global plagues and the like, filing one's taxes, however important a task, seems not terribly serious at all, maybe even trivial in comparison. Or the situation in the Middle East, no one's going to call that anything less than serious, extremely serious. More than just a pencil and an old calculator are going to be needed to work that out. No accountant, not even a team of highly accomplished and talented accountants is up that level of seriousness. He looks at his pencil where it lay on a paperback book across the room and laughs, imagining the team of accountants staggered by the depth and complexity of the situation in the Middle East and the realization that the work to which they have for years assiduously dedicated themselves was never truly serious at all. It would be no surprise if they wept at that moment, those talented accountants, watching the sun set in the Middle East. That moment itself could be fairly termed serious, maybe the most serious moment of their lives. None of the hours of determining deductibles and exemptions, even taken as a mighty sum, could compare with that moment. One might even envy them that moment. Call it seriousness envy.

He has not, on this occasion, this spring, yet cleared the dining room table and brought out the stacks of bills and calculator and pencil. And he does not know why, and that seems strange to him, especially now, having reflected on how serious, fairly serious, he understands the filing of taxes to be, though it has occurred to him that in truth perhaps he does not take it as seriously as all that, given the comparisons with massive oil spills and earthquakes and chronic heart trouble, all of a quite different scale of seriousness. In fact it was in conversation with his brother that the subject had arisen: his brother had asked him, on the phone, whether he had filed his taxes yet, a question which probably held no genuine interest for him but which he was in all likelihood asking because he knew or suspected that his brother took the matter seriously, seriously enough to be remarked upon. He cannot remember telling his brother about his attitude to income tax but it was not necessarily the sort of thing that he would remember, whereas his brother, having been in and out of hospitals so often in recent years and in the process subjected to so many shallow conversations with visitors looking in on him, might well have seized upon anything said to him in those exchanges and turned the words over and over in mind. It might well be to a man in yet another hospital bed, wondering whether this hospital bed could be his last hospital bed, that not only does the filing of taxes seem anything but serious, the notion that a healthy man such as his brother, able to walk in and out of a hospital at his leisure, takes his tax reporting seriously, even fairly or moderately seriously, is preposterous, incomprehensible. Maybe even contemptible. In which case the question on the phone, have you done your taxes yet, was no innocuous, polite way of shuffling along in conversation, the way so many of their conversations shuffled along, but something else: a jibe, as though to mock his poor appreciation of the elements of his life. This thought stung him. He is suddenly of half a mind not to do his taxes this year, to let the government deadline slip by, and when next on the phone with his brother let him know, waiting for his brother to ask his loaded question, to dangle his baited hook once more and then feigning an absent mind and asking in return, what, the deadline has passed, oh well, it's not serious. Or he might just announce it: do you know what, I didn't file my taxes at all, I just can't take such little things seriously.

Of course that's not what he would do, even if it were the case that he was being needled by his brother. In fact if anybody isn't taking their affairs seriously it is his brother, judging from the number of times he has had to be raced to this or that hospital. Bad diet, lack of exercise, these it turns out are serious in their own way. When he had been listening to that doctor outside his brother's room in the hospital, the second time in that second hospital, she had given some technical explanations that he had not been entirely able to follow, arrhythmia was the word she repeated, and he had thought to himself: *arrhythmia, arrhythmia*. He was trying to take the whole business seriously but a sense of hilarity was breaking in: this second time in this hospital, all over again, and here was this doctor with the most pointy nose ever seen, a dangerous weapon, and she kept saying *arrhythmia, arrhythmia* to him, and he dreaded each time she would say it again, *arrhythmia, arrhythmia*, breathily like that, because he did not want to laugh, because he could see this was serious. If only his brother had taken nutrition and exercise seriously, this dagger-faced doctor would not have to chant *arrhythmia, arrhythmia* at him. He had refrained from telling his brother the details about that encounter when they were talking, him seated beside his brother's hospital bed, the latest in a series of hospital beds. In fact it was possible that it was during that very conversation, when he conscientiously omitted the sharp nose of the doctor and her breathy *arrhythmia, arrhythmia* that he made mention, maybe as a kind of nonchalant way of not discussing the doctor's nose, of his thoughts on doing one's taxes. Unlikely, but possible.

Again he thinks of, and pictures vividly, the weeping accountants. If only they could quantify and compute their despair. If only there were a kind of emotional tax return that everyone could file annually, listing experiences and encounters and thoughts that had affected them in some way, from fleeting bemusement to enduring horror and everything in between. Of course the government would not be able to offer, as it were, emotional reimbursements, some sort of supplementary or compensatory dosage of happiness, but the exercise of carefully filing such a return might very well prove of no small benefit, providing helpful perspective to the authors of their respective returns as well as to the government accountants and bureaucrats, who would be effectively freed from the narrow, abstract understanding of the citizenry as gross and net incomes and differing arrangements of credits and exemptions, and thereafter irreversibly aware of them as complex and changeable, fierce and fragile psychologies. He likes the idea. He can barely imagine just how radically tax accountants would be transformed. There would be no jokes about dull accountants after that. It would be a more serious job than any other. And ultimately the situation in the Middle East might be worked out by this new kind of accountants, accountants who could produce a comprehensive emotional assessment of all of the parties involved and calculate what is owed to or from whom in the fairest manner possible.

He likes the idea, call it a harmless fantasy, but he can only guess what his brother would make of it, especially if that seemingly innocuous question about whether he has done his taxes yet was not so innocuous after all. He gets up from his chair and moves to watch the rain at the window. Unimpressive weather. The kind of day that might be given over to some unglamourous chore. He thinks about the cost of replacing the furnace. He thinks about what a strange contraption the heart is, the whole circulation system actually, all of it so bizarre. At any given moment all of that blood thoughtlessly flowing through him, some of it fully oxygenated, on its way to this or that extremity, while some of it returns, depleted, to the pump: exhausting just to think of it, though of course exhausting is the wrong word, a respiratory word, when what's wanted is a sanguinary word. Involuntarily he speaks aloud huskily: *arrhythmia, arrhythmia*. Not the right word at all, of course. This is the side of himself he somehow never showed his brother, this unserious and idle side of himself, the side of him that stares at the rain and conjures up harmless fantasies when he could and in fact by rights should be taking the opportunity to get his taxes out of the way. Maybe very few people ever glimpsed this side of him. He wonders whether this might be so, whether people tended to think him a man taken up with seriousness, with serious things, incapable of fancy, altogether incapable of dreaming up an inventive solution to any of life's little problems, let alone the situation in the Middle East.

He could write a letter to, say, the Ministry of Revenue, even the Minister himself, and outline his idea. He scratches his chin, not because it ever itched but because it was something he habitually did when he thought he was being crafty. Dear Minister, in the course of filing my taxes this year, he might begin, though that would be stretching the truth a little, for he was hardly in the course of it, no sign yet of the stacks of bills and the calculator, and the pencil was still sitting atop the paperback in which it had been used to underline a passage. Dear Minister, I am sure that you are painfully aware of how soulless the business of filing one's taxes is thought to be by so much of the population. Laying it on pretty thick there, as his brother would say. That must be a painting expression, though his brother has never demonstrated any interest in painting. Dear Minister, seeing as the revenue service is in a sense the heart of the government, it ought to model itself on a heart, pumping oxygenated blood, which is to say measures of happiness, to those parts of the body that need it, just as the depleted blood, the anxiety and tedium and sometimes the sorrow that come wrapped up in annual tax returns, come for your examination and rejuvenation. Who is the Minister of Revenue? He tried to picture him but for some reason could only picture a chittering dolphin. A kind of association, that might be: perhaps the Minister's name was something like dolphin. Or porpoise. Or mereswine. Or perhaps not. In fact writing such a letter would probably be crossing the line from harmless fantasy into outright crankery. He might find himself in a hospital, with poor odds of it being the same hospital as his brother.

It is still raining and he is still at the window watching it rain. None of the descriptions of rain that he has ever known of, none of the feelings often associated with rain struck him as right. Rain is not sad or depressing. Nor is it refreshing. It does not portend anything. It is part of a cycle, that's all. Rain is not serious: in fact, that is what rain could be summed up as, not an event or a symbol but a disavowal of seriousness. It is raining, it is not serious. And that might seem comforting but on further reflection anyone would realize that it's not especially comforting, for it is only not serious for as long as it rains, and besides there are good reasons to want seriousness. Doing one's taxes has a seriousness, however negligible when compared with earthquakes and highway accidents and yes, *arrhythmia, arrhythmia*, but the rain just rains, one drop after another. A circulatory system. It was all very well for some people not to take things seriously, with bad diets and no exercise and failing to complete a full tax return each year, but where did that lead, was there a purpose, purpose and not porpoise, oh no, it led nowhere, hospital after hospital, shallow conversation after shallow conversation, round and round. He did not hire an accountant, he never hired an accountant, he did his taxes every year by himself, just a matter of patience and arithmetic, he took it seriously and did it himself. That meant something. He would do it again this year as he had every other year, after clearing off the dining table and bringing the pencil and the calculator and the stacks of bills to the table and going through it once, twice, one more time. That's what he would do.

DISCOVERY AND PATIENCE

My father discovered the Aztecs when he was not yet twenty years old. There were five of them, hiding behind the hockey arena — the old arena, that is, not the new one. The new one was just what the taxpayers were clamoring for, you can't have too many arenas. Well, these Aztecs were not up to much, but of course my father didn't know that then, and his thoughts were all filled with human sacrifice and so on.

He received no prizes or accolades for this discovery, but he was not bitter. Nor was he bitter when the government ignored his many warnings about the insidious replacement of the moon with a device disguised as the moon. Together we would sit outside of this or that office, his briefcase between his feet, his palms pressed gently together in front of him. Patience. And nights, when he thought I was asleep in bed, I watched him staring into the fireplace, above which hung his own meticulously drawn, painted, and annotated map of the world. His fingers would touch, but he did not want to use, the silver whistle hung as a pendant round his neck, the whistle given to him by his friend the Queen of Dinosaurs.

Patience. There is no crisis that cannot be surmounted.

Blowing this whistle would summon whatever dinosaurs might prove most helpful at that moment, such as, for example, a pterodactyl to swoop down suddenly and carry him to safety, if that was what was required, but my father had promised his friend the Queen of Dinosaurs that he would only use the whistle in the most dire emergency, so as not to draw the few yet remaining dinosaurs from their hiding places.

Where has that silver whistle gotten to now, I'd quite like to know.

NO HARM IN ASKING

And it was true that she had gone out with the Sublime for a while. In fact, they were briefly engaged to be married. Everybody was always asking her what it was like. How did they meet? It was on a trip to see the ocean; she had suddenly needed time to herself and wanted to take in as much fresh air as possible, widen the horizon. And there she was, looking out at the Pacific, and a voice beside her said exactly what she was thinking at the moment: *Impossible to take it all in.* She smiled before turning her head and there was the Sublime, offering her pretzels from a bag. She sometimes liked to dazzle her friends with that detail: *the Sublime is dead nuts on pretzels.* Really? Could produce a bag of them at the most unlikely occasion. And that had admittedly charmed her. But a pretzel is just a tidbit, a salty tease, and they wanted more, but usually didn't know how to ask, probably in large part because they didn't quite know what they wanted to know. Just more. What did they do together, she and the Sublime? She would look at her questioners, hands on large lattes, boutique bags at their feet, just back from a purchase of eyebrows with artificial intelligence. Did they want to know about the failed apple strudel experiment, the sock fights that broke out in the midst of laundry afternoons, the unresolved argument about whether to adopt a cat or a dog? More. If they want to know about sex, let them ask about sex, and if they ask about sex, let them wait until they have to ask something else. But, but, but the engagement, how did that get called off? Had she been disappointed, or was it a case of the one who got away? Shaking the head. How could she have possibly managed to say *I do*, how could that have ever had any genuine meaning? What could it mean to say *I do* to the Sublime, with the Sublime standing right there, right there? But nobody wants such questions in response to their questions, down-to-earth questions answered with head-in-the-clouds-questions. She quickly learned not to bother trying. Their intelligent eyebrows arch, adjust to the best light, bristle, thrust, parry, project beautiful patience. Instead she would reply, with a small laugh meant to suggest anything they wanted it to, *Oh, it was the whole pretzel thing. Crunching on them all the time. It was more than I could take.*

THE BORES

Of course I know, as we all do, many people we may rightly call bores. So many such people, and they are everywhere. They are eating in good restaurants, comparing this stamp with that one in the post office, browsing shelves in the library, waiting for their flight to be announced in the airport lounge, and talking, it goes without saying, in all these places and at all times they are talking. They all have their subjects, their preoccupations, their fixations, and this is how they are recognized and more or less conveniently classified.

There are, for example, the wine bore, the stereo equipment bore, the political intrigue bore, the sports statistics bore, the public transit schedule bore, the gardening bore, the occult societies bore, and the weather bore. Or there are the marriage advisor bore, the real estate bore, the etymology bore, the interior design bore, the infectious disease bore, the jazz bore, the well travelled bore, the military history bore, the fitness bore, the stock market bore. And let's not forget the photography bore, the childhood trauma bore, the horse bore, the lunar landing bore, the family lineage bore, the bicycling bore, the state of today's education bore, the forgotten celebrities bore, the difficult allergies bore, the natural disaster bore, and so many others. It is diverting to wonder whether there are more subjects readily appropriate for bores than there are those that are not, or even whether any such distinction holds.

By and large the bores are self-taught and enjoy telling the story of that education — or, if perhaps they do not really enjoy it, they cannot help themselves. Just think of that: a driving compulsion to hold fast to people, the way a snake coils around and hypnotizes its prey. But eventually a snake strikes and feeds. The bores never do that: there is no endgame, no climax, and probably no satiety (perhaps only a bore would want to ascertain that).

Bores can be found everywhere, but especially in places designated for waiting or where there is relatively little movement. A party is a natural example of the latter: perhaps despite themselves, parties escalate the chances of an encounter with a bore or two. A wedding is practically a guarantee.

At one wedding a few years ago, I was a university classmate of the bride, not a long-time or especially close friend but a friend from a recent-enough cherished time, and so I was assigned a seat a couple of tables away from the inner circle. While I had thought it wise to bring a date, the friend I imposed this duty on was repeatedly taking himself outside for a cigarette or to take yet another phone call. This left me all too open to the conversation of the dateless man seated next to me.

Complaining about the food is a safe approach, though I noticed that he left nothing on each plate as it was taken away. He bulged out of his worn suit and wore glasses that made his face seem even bigger than it was. He spoke slowly, the clear result of an ongoing conflict between satisfaction with his ideas and some distrust of the words he was using, as though they might be getting into trouble without his knowing. He had a bird's nest beard and thick lips that together conspired to slow his pasty speech even further.

Determining what connection he had with the parties getting married was "complicated," and that word was the first warning. Though he didn't really know the bride, it turned out that she had the same last name as a librarian he used to know, back when he used to go to that library, before it conjured up new and ridiculous rules for its patrons. Apparently the bride and this librarian were cousins, or at least he was eighty-nine percent sure of that, but he had never spoken to the bride before that day's ceremony. So no, not exactly a close friend of the groom's either, more along the lines of a family friend, you might say, though it had nothing to do with bloodlines or marriage. The groom's stepmother he had known for a number of years, it must be ten or twelve.

There was something about a car accident and something else about insurance, or insurance fraud. My attention had begun to wander at this point. He might have said that he had considered studying law, or perhaps had studied it for a little while, and he explained that justice was a concept too elusive event to talk about, and he reviewed the decline of education and unnecessary airport procedures and government corruption and Pier Paolo Pasolini. The victim of a bore will almost always seize upon something so specific and tangible as a proper name in hopes of attaining some focus. Pasolini? The judgment on Pasolini was extensive. I managed to interrupt its course only with a diversionary question: you're interested in movies, then?

More than interested: he was a filmmaker; he was working on a film. How long had he been working on it? Eleven years. Eleven years (one feels compelled to repeat it), that's quite a long time (one feels compelled to comment).

"This kind of film I am working on," he said with extra slowness, "is not a mainstream kind of film."

The kind of film he was working on was not a mainstream kind of film.

If wedding speeches have any saving grace, it is that they may rescue us from such conversations, and as soon as the final toasts were made I excused myself, found the toilets and there thought about my life. Picky picky, my mother's refrain throughout my life: that's the reason why these situations happen, why you are the sociologist of the bores, why you are single. But it couldn't be the whole reason. Is there some scent or pheromone that attracts bores? And where was that date of mine, who had been last seen with phone in one hand and lighter in the other?

I walked around the banquet hall, unambitiously looking for him and toying with the idea of calling a taxi. The Headache Orchestra was unmistakeably tuning up for a performance. The open bar politely suggested that another glass of wine might rain it out. The bartender seemed pleased not be dealing with someone ordering five different drinks. Somebody in line was telling a story about the groom's father of which I only heard "and then the minute they were in the water, chugga-chugga-chugga." This made the two women beside me vie to outdo each other's shrieking laughter, which the ever-eager Orchestra gladly took as a cue.

I drifted from the bar and to my right I noticed two men talking in the corridor — or rather, two men ostensibly in dialogue, though it became quickly apparent that one was doing most of the talking and the other barely offering an occasional phrase. The latter was a well-dressed man, perhaps less than medium height, whose sense of composure radiated out of him. The bulky figure I recognized as the man who was working on a film that was not a mainstream kind of film. Rocking back and forth from one foot to the other, he was in effect blocking the corridor. The hands of the smaller man signalled in a way that seemed polite but definite an intention to walk past, but the larger man disregarded this, unmistakably carrying on his slow monologue.

What happened next was so sudden that I hardly know how to describe it. The well-dressed man leaned down and across, as though he were touching the other man's left toe with his right hand, and then his left hand came up and touched the other man's right shoulder. Of these movements I am fairly certain, but the subsequent crisscrossing of these rapid, light-fingered grabs occurred faster than I could follow with either my eyes or understanding. Even had I been capable of recognizing each movement as discreet and intelligible, my senses were overfilled with an even more incomprehensible phenomenon: The man who was working on a film that was not a mainstream kind of film was being folded up, folded up into an ever smaller parcel. There was not a moment allowed him even to think of resisting. In two heartbeats the bore was reduced to a tiny rectangle no larger than a matchbook, which the well-dressed man turned over in his left hand. He coolly examined it for a moment before slipping it into one of the large potted ficuses in the corridor. As he stepped in my direction he looked directly into my face and, without changing his easy pace, approached me.

"It was Byron, I think, who said that there are only two mighty tribes, the Bores and the Bored." He adjusted the handkerchief winking from his jacket. "Careful, you're about to spill your wine."

His name was Oran. There is no precise antonym for the category of bore, let alone Bore. I have gradually come to think that this is right, that it is as it should be. Still, if there were such a term, it would apply to Oran. Only an hour after meeting him did I realize that he silenced the Orchestra, a feat unmatched by any individual.

I have left out, from my earlier list, the sex bore and the love bore. Both are exquisitely awful but they are special because they do not deal in pure boredom: they spike their offerings with different kinds and degrees of discomfort and disgust. Other kinds of bore depend upon the civility of others, but the sex bore and the love bore also make direct appeal to the human needs and weaknesses of their listeners. To the world travel bore, it doesn't matter at all whether the listener has the slightest interest in the relative merits of this or that cruise liner, or novel solutions to passport difficulties, but the sex bore is assured of attention because sex is the fulcrum to the see-saw between titillation and disgust. The encounter with the love bore is a more complicated (and less reliable) sort of amusement park ride, with the potential for excitement, disappointment, and disaster at every turn.

But you see how this works, and now you naturally wonder whether I became, that night and the nights that followed in Oran's hotel room, one of these kinds of bores, never mind which. And the thing is I can't decide or taxonomize myself; it's probably not up to me to do so. The best that I can do is acknowledge the fact as briefly as I can and thereafter focus elsewhere.

"How did you do it?" I asked him, while my hands did something to his something.

He did something in response. "You don't mean this."

I somethinged a little but persevered: "To the bore. At the reception. I don't think I imagined it."

His teacher, he said, had explained it this way: to understand *origami* as a martial art is no more imaginative than it is simply logical. It is all about locating angles and points, motions and force, and redirecting these where necessary and possible. His teacher said it might be called *orinyūsansu*, but since its whole purpose was to bring restful silence, it might be better not to name it anything at all.

"It is actually a simple art, and that's the source of its elegance. But it is also obviously a powerful art, and that is the reason for its secrecy. Very few know of it at all, and far fewer are those who practice it."

It may be because I am a bad person, or it may be because Oran's something had engulfed my something, but I did not ask what the effect was on the man who was working on a film that was not a mainstream kind of film, or whether he would ever emerge from that compressed state. Instead I asked, "Can you teach me?"

His watchful, amused look did not waver that first night.

Nor did it any of the other nights. "Why would you want to learn?"

"To be among neither of the tribes." I told him about the bores, all the bores I had dealt with, and about sometimes feeling like a lightning rod for them. As he listened, Oran stopped somethinging my something something.

No, he could not teach me. He was no teacher, it took many years to acquire any skill at all, and in any event, he was only in town for the wedding, and would be leaving the country within the week. His eyes were something, really something, at that moment, and part of me wanted to kill him but it was outvoted by all of my other parts, which were enthralled.

And I stayed enthralled, but on our last night I asked again if he would teach me to defend myself with *orinyūsansu*. His smile flickered. Again he said no, but he paused before answering and then paused again, longer this time, before adding, "but perhaps there is another option."

He gestured for me to stand and we faced each other naked, that much I remember. He then asked me to remain completely still. "I will speak to you. Listen for my voice." Only in the moment before he thrust his fingers to the tip of my ear did it occur to me to have doubts. Who was this man, besides terrific evening pastime and the possessor of a knowledge and skill that I coveted? Formulating questions about how far I might trust him took longer than it did for him to fold me: there's the ceiling,

there's the bottom of my foot,
there's his hand,
there's my lower back, his hand, the ceiling,

there's what
what
where.

"Listen to my voice, focus on what I'm telling you now. Origami, which you may know about, is the changing of shapes, not of substance. The paper assumes the form of a star, a tiger, a ship, but it is always paper. We are not changing the substance of you, but we are changing your shape."

What is
that looks like
but
the ceiling
coming down

"Listen to my voice. Your senses are part of your shape: how you see, how you hear, how you feel the world around you. Folding changes the shape, creating corners and curves that were not there before, introducing apertures and closing others. My hands are looking for the senses that are affected by the bores you complain of."

His hands
coming down
I am, I'm in
his hands

"These are very tiny folds I am making now, the slightest adjustments, and though as I say your substance will not be changed, your shape and form as a whole will as a consequence. If we do this just right, you will be less vulnerable to the effects of these people, because you will not hear them as well as you do now, but on the other hand, if I may use that expression, you will notice them more readily and at a greater distance, before they get near. Now this is the trickiest part here."

whoa whoa whoa

what the ceiling what the

where are you his

hands up now up

I am

up

I'm

momentarily standing, breathless, and then fallen onto the bed, gasping. The curtains had changed their colour or they had not changed their colour but I was unable to resolve the question. The curtains were aloof, aslant. The curtains were asleep. I was asleep.

Later I was awake. Predictably. And alone, also predictably. (Picky picky, I know.)

Oran I never saw or heard from again. He would be "leaving the country," he said, and we did not, amid all the somethinging of somethings, speak of destinations. Or of plans, of contact information.

The days (the months) go by the same and the air tastes no different, though maybe I'm wrong. My mother says that I've changed but she won't be more specific. A few weeks ago I was at a party and almost no one spoke to me, not even the guy who was unmistakeably a cognitive therapy bore. I stayed longer than I should have and went home with the assurance of a headache the next morning: the Orchestra had not left me, and it wanted me to sense its devotion. For its part, my apartment's greeting was not effusive, and my mattress seemed to sigh even before I laid down. It is terrible not knowing exactly what you want, and still knowing that you can't have it. "Careful, you're about to spill your wine," I said aloud. And I replied, because the apartment could not: "Careful, you're becoming a bore."

THE DAY BEFORE SHE

She set the photo album on the side table, not thinking about how it somehow never managed to return to the shelf these days (why was that?), and crossed to the ringing phone. An unfamiliar voice, older and with crisp, almost forced articulation, asked for her by name. She said, "Yes, this is she."

"Look here," the voice said, "I have a few things to say about your cookbook, the most recent one. How you can bear to have your name on such a book, I'll never understand. It's terrible, honestly terrible. I must have tried a dozen recipes, all of them disasters, before I gave up."

She did not even consider interrupting (why was that?).

"Incorrect portions, sloppy composition, both in the dishes and the writing, come to that. Your previous cookbooks, they were bad, but this one is dreadful, terrible. Honestly. Nothing I tried making from it worked out. The pictures bear no resemblance. And you have no idea," and the voice quavered, rising higher than perhaps it had planned, with no way of going back, "no idea what it feels like to feel cheated after so much work, even as I allowed for the level of incompetence and disappointment I've come to expect in dealing with these books of yours, these exceptionally bad books. Even some of the ingredients are irresponsibly chosen, fashionable and expensive and rare bagatelles and bits of nothing put in to seem *au courant*." The voice sounded as though it came from a throat held in a tight, perhaps squeezing grip, which acted as a monitoring influence, holding back certain words, checking emotion as best it might.

There was a pause in which neither spoke.

"Well," she offered.

"Disaster after disaster. It is one thing to be dull and bad, as you well know your other books are, but this one, this one is *unforgivable*."

There was a clicking sound and for a moment she had thought the caller had hung up, but then the voice said, "That's all I have to say," and, after another moment, "Goodbye," and a more definitive click followed.

She set the phone down and lit the burner under the kettle. The different teas were arranged in a special order. Not alphabetical order or by region: a personal logic was at work, but it was a logic of some time ago, strange to her now.

"The drinking of tea is an escape from time's passing."

If there had been a pet in the house, a cat, for instance, it would have looked up and so alerted her to the fact the she had spoken this aloud (why was that?). The alerted look of such a cat or other animal might have acted as a friendly but firm statement of contradiction: no, it isn't, it is a cup of tea, and there is no such escape.

And then all at once it was late afternoon. She was frowning at the simmering stock, or was it simmering at the frowning stock, in her hand a glass of Chardonnay with two gulps left. With her other hand she picked up the ringing frowning simmering phone.

This voice was male, in the sense that it wanted that matter clear. It also asked for her by name.

"Speaking," she said.

"I am sorry to disturb you," sounding authentically apologetic, "and I realize that you don't know me."

"No," she said, being helpful (why was that?).

"My name is . . . Well, I don't suppose that really matters. The thing is, I am afraid that my wife may have called you earlier today, and really gave you an earful. You don't need to confirm it, I know that she did. We try to keep her away from making these calls, but one can't watch her every moment and sometimes she manages to get to a phone. And she makes these calls to people, all sorts of people, you wouldn't believe. Any chance she gets, calling the most unpredictable people. She managed to call this television weatherman, that was the first one that we know of, and really let him have it. He cheated her out of a nice weekend, he was an outrageous liar, ought to be locked up, that sort of thing. There have been librarians and mortuaries and the editor of a fashion magazine. A couple of months ago it was embassies: the Italian embassy, the German embassy, the Lithuanian embassy. Not to mention the neighbours, anybody at all. And I have to call back, like I'm doing now, to apologize and explain, like I'm doing now." He seemed to realize he had to slow down. "So yes, yes, I'm deeply apologetic for that call. I must ask you to forgive her. I don't know exactly what she said to you when she called, but believe me I know the kind of thing. She can be really blistering, merciless."

She looked through the kitchen door to the couch where lay open the photo album. It was always open. Was that a stain on the couch, or a trick of the light? What could have caused it? There were reasons for things, there were always reasons.

"She picks people to call up, people she doesn't know at all, I really have no idea how she manages to get their numbers. She calls them up and runs them down something awful. I don't know what she said to you, of course. But she's not well. That's just it, she's not well and I really am very sorry that you had to endure that," he sought the word, "that abuse."

She felt sure she was going to say "I appreciate your calling," but halted at "appreciate."

This response decomposed him only a little. "Yes, so yes, that's very good of you. There was a time," she heard him lick his lips or run his hand over his mouth, "a time when my wife would have said as much. She used to have excellent manners, she was really a very social person, much more than I am. But now, well. We have to watch her. We have to watch her very carefully."

She began to frame a question, "Is she . . ." but the call was over.

The soup was not restorative, but fine. Evening took over. She turned on the radio and heard a little Mendelssohn, she thought it was, but shut it off after only a few minutes. The kitchen was clean so she did not have to clean it, but she inspected it nonetheless. A troublesome stuck drawer caught her attention and for a while she fussed over and banged away at it, eventually opting to empty it and take it out. Something was jamming the left track. The hall clock rang eight times and when it was done the phone rang.

She set the drawer on the floor and waited through the second ring, the third ring, and then stood up.

"Hello?"

No voice answered. She stood waiting, determined to wait. There was somebody on the line.

"Hello?"

There were reasons for things. There always were. Her cheeks burned under the mute stares of the faces in the photo album and the cat and everyone else who wasn't there.

WHEN THE SEALS
WOULD CLAP NO MORE

If it seems unusual to discover a preface appended to an object that is all too often called a "colouring book," perhaps prejudices have become unguardedly confused with expectations. There is sometimes urgency in the unexpected. Therefore be warned: despite its innocuous-seeming charms (that it only seems innocuous is one of its charms), *Join the Circus!* is no ordinary bound stack of paper to be idly defaced, and this preface is likely to disturb and distress those who underestimate what they have opened.

Join the Circus! is certainly a joy to behold — *to behold*, it must be stressed and not *to lay wax upon willy-nilly*. The narrative that the keen-eyed reader can puzzle together from the sequence of tableaux is simple, concise, sometimes slyly allusive, and genuinely moving. It needs no improvement. The intersecting circles of clowns and poodles on page 11 are utterly dynamic precisely because they arc in black and white, because the artist who gave them exuberant life disdained the superfluous and focussed on the power of the line. Reddening these clowns' noses will not make them more antic: such an assault would irretrievably lose all the picture's mirth. The facial expression of the poodle in the right corner is nothing less than haunting, but the smallest smear of pink, say, would demolish that nuance. The whole essence of the clown's nose, the poodle's ineffable expression would be violated.

Exaggeration? No. No and again no. We must understand *Join the Circus!* rather than disfigure it. No one would countenance a gluing together of various pages of the Gnostic gospels or the Analects of Confucius, or fecklessly stand by as some cheerful maniac made paper dolls out of *The Origin of Species* or *The Last Bandstand: An Unbiased Argument Against the Use of the Conductor's Baton.* These claims need not even be made — the renown of such wonders defends them; and yet one must even today defend *Join the Circus!*

Why? Regard, for example, the illustration on page 7: the juggling bear on the unicycle. The temptation here might be to juxtapose merry brown for the animal's fur with jaunty red for the fez, but to do so would be a mistake. Why? For one thing, there is the temerity of asserting the familiar: bears may frequently have brown coats, but there is no reason to suppose that this particular, splendid specimen (capable of juggling four balls while riding a unicycle, a feat which the reader is politely invited to match — without opposable thumbs) does not have a magenta coat. This is only one kind of error, however. The zany who, for the sake of unconventionality or as wearisome "avant-garde" gesture, scoops up the forest green crayon to colour only the bear's left side and polka dots the right in orange presumes both that the colour does not matter and that his or her "artistic licence" trumps all other possible contingencies and concerns. Imagine a surgeon who announced, hands still within the patient's open cavity, "this organ would look much better over here." Imagine the firefighter who aims the arcs of hosed water right over the blazing homestead, with the justification that to his eye it looks more pleasing than merely dousing the flames directly. Just imagine!

These rhetorical examples are to some extent misleading, however; for it is not a question of how to do something (what is the right colour for the bear's delightful fez) but whether to do it at all, and the answer, as this preface aims to make abundantly clear, is no. Unless one has a comprehensive grasp of a work, it is not only impertinent but hazardous to meddle with it. Why is the aforementioned bear juggling four balls, and not three, or five? Why does one of the creases in its tutu seem out of place, as though pointing to some vanished vanishing point? What is the significance of the ringmaster's moustache on page 4, or the significance of its apparent absence only five pages later (see the back left corner, where the ringmaster appears to be levitating)? Whose is that supernumerary shadow behind the bearded lady on page 2? The lion at the furthest left on page 10 seems to wink at the reader, but to what purpose? These questions and puzzles, of which there are many, should stay the hand that would thoughtlessly "fill in" what may only seem to be blanks.

One pales at the thought of the pornographic device used by stage illusionists, showing to the approving audience an untouched volume of these kinds of line drawings (though few match those of *Join the Circus!*) before waving a silly wand and revealing how the book has been thoroughly despoiled with thick, insipid colours. When we think of such acts we better respect the way our forebears dispatched those who practised such arts. If terrorists were to smirch the Colosseum in gaudy paint, there would be an outcry for hard and swift justice, and rightly so. The case here is even more grave, both because this book is so much more vulnerable than monuments that already have won international recognition and protection, and because, as has already been hinted, the depths of *Join the Circus!* have yet to be plumbed.

A brief introduction such as this can only trace where these depths begin to descend. Close examination of the hair of the female trapezist on page 3 reveals a pattern of parallel waves that very closely resemble the song patterns of humpback whales. (This has been confirmed by witnesses.) The cetological connection points to two other unexpected links: first, the absence of any aquatic life (including performing seals!) in *Join the Circus!*; and second, the name of Giacomo Spermaceti, author of the aforementioned volume *The Last Bandstand: An Unbiased Argument Against the Use of the Conductor's Baton*. Spermaceti drowned, quite possibly a suicide, in a public aquarium, only a few months after the completion of his seminal book, but it may be conceivable that the unknown artist behind *Join the Circus!* has absorbed some of the unreleased energies of the man who once wrote that "the only destiny worth recognizing can be heard in the applause of an audience that is not there" and in these pages channels them. Pause to consider what happens if that hair streaking out behind her were suddenly yellowed, browned, or blued: what vital networks of illumination are suddenly dashed away. How fragile a thing is wonder.

As fragile as life itself, one might answer with Spermaceti's sad life, or what we know of it, in mind. His parents arrived in Montreal with the young boy, probably aged two, and a single suitcase, surprised to find that it was not an American city. This troubled sense of geography seems to have been passed on to their son, whose unpublished journal makes references to India as the Middle East, Cuba as a South American island, and Moscow as a city in Iceland. Even his masterpiece (and only published work), *The Last Bandstand*, refers to Italy as "easily the largest country in Western Europe" and to Madagascar as "the sumptuous capital of Morocco." It is worth remembering that circuses as a rule do not have a fixed address, a point which only adds to the fascinating connections between the book you now hold in your hands and the neglected author who was probably the first to note that batons are inhuman supplements for the human finger.

According to the creditors who knew him best, Spermaceti had his first genuine experience of music when he was about four years old, at a park bandstand: a Sousa march. It made him dizzy and unable to move, and that began his extensive medical history with specialists trying to figure out what had happened to him. His mother was not assured when his hearing was found to be normal and his reactions to recordings of Sousa (and of several other kinds of music) impassive and unremarkable. She depleted the family savings taking the boy from expert to expert, from clinic to clinic, until the unorthodox psychologist Karmosin Skottkärra from Stockholm expressed interest in the case. Skottkärra cannily suggested that the trigger for the boy's catatonia was not auditory but visual: the answer lay in something he saw in the performance. A new series of tests, isolating different musical instruments in order to eliminate them, seemed to lead nowhere until — but here we come to familiar history: the obsessive years of study, the neglect of the manuscript, that terrible sunny afternoon at the aquarium, the posthumous publication and dissemination, all known. This is how a terrible but imminent purpose overtakes one, even at a tender age, even manifested in what might seem an utterly trivial phenomenon, and becomes a driving force ultimately for the benefit of others, and of posterity, too.

What hue best captures this life of despair and uncertainty? How can a small box representing such a narrow spectrum encompass what it means to be thus possessed, thrust into the world with pain and the knowledge that one must not only identify this pain precisely, but to share and spread as widely as possible one's researches, for this pain cannot be unique and the world will be better for knowing the source of this obscure but haunting pain, that everyone might join together to make it stop?

Spouses and friends may not understand *Join the Circus!* — or, indeed, the zealous commitment that it requires. Children may and likely shall wail no matter how patiently it is explained to them that the human cannonball (the climactic page 14) is flying through the air towards something greater than they can understand, and their proposed imposition of rainbows will only yank him crashing down to the ground. Employers, publishers, and members of the judiciary may frown. Open your eyes and see: see how that lion winks at you — at you — and know that this is a call for reading between the lines rather than, as some lunatic has coined the phrase, staying within them. Look and look again, and applaud the wonders of this extraordinary, untouchable circus.

This book is yours now, to cherish and to protect.

EVERYBODY'S SORRY

"Just try them on."

"I like the other ones better."

"Yes, I know, but you've already heard me tell you twice that they don't have those ones in your size and you badly need a new pair of shoes for school. Come on, Ducks, help me out here. Try them on and we can look at some others."

It was almost another half an hour by the time they got to the cash register with a box and promises that the truculent little thing would wear the chosen shoes. Would she make it to the bank before it closed, and who was it she was supposed to call today? Her mind, her mind. Nobody to call for that.

"Amber?"

She looked at the woman who had addressed her. Forty-something, hair dyed with autumnal streaks, wearing the Shoe Depot apron and a tremendous smile. She only recognized Rose, Rose Surname with a P, when she announced her name, and then found within the face the traits of a younger, slimmer face she once knew. In the last years of high school they had not been friends, exactly, but very much the friends of friends, almost always at the same parties. The same orbit, but that sounds like there was a common centre of gravity, which there likely never was.

"I had no idea you lived in town."

"That crazy little thing called work."

"Hey," said Rose, thumbing her apron's strap. "The things we do."

No ring, so Amber decided not to ask, and she sees Rose make the same calculation. They agreed that the town's not so bad; in fact better in some ways than it used to be.

"Hand out of your mouth, Ducks, I know you're hungry." She had to pull the offending hand away herself. The scanner was cheerfully beeping prices, a mating call to credit cards, and the conversation was keeping the beat.

"Don't get out much because of Dad," Rose's long black earrings were flashing. "There's a nurse with him in the days while I'm working but."

The shoes were bought, both pairs, and their indifferent owner's mother had something to do Friday night.

II

She found the house without difficulty: a semi-detached with Christmas lights still in evidence. Rose, in a dress, opened the door before Amber reached for the bell.

"Dad's asleep," she giggled. Too much. Par something not Parker or Partridge. But the stifled giggle brought back the adolescent to Rose's mind, making the same gesture at a pool party after someone had been pushed in: wild glee checked by something between remorse and uncertainty.

The small living room smelled of furniture polish and the carpet bore the imprints of recent and vigorous vacuuming. On the far wall were mounted the descending white commands

LIVE

    LOVE

       LAUGH

"I've got wine, red or white as you prefer. I've also got Wild Turkey and even a bottle of our old Mexican friend if we decide to let things get crazy."

The wine was better than Amber had expected. Rose refilled their glasses before they were half empty. Amber explained that she had not long ago landed a job at a small publisher of children's books, though it was at this point still contract work. Each acknowledged a failed marriage but did not dwell on it. They remembered Amy and Gina and Nikki Waterson and Troy Rhodes. They laughed about Dwayne the Pain and about the night of the flying fish and about the open patio doors at the Reynolds' house.

"I thought the whole neighbourhood knew what was going on that night."

"All I remember is that nobody stuck around to find out."

"You know what we should do? Do you know what I do now and then?"

Amber smiled at the girlish excitement, shook her head.

"Get high," said Rose. "We could get really high."

"Oh, I didn't expect you to say that."

"We could get really high." Rose squeezed her legs together in excitement and wobbled on her seat. "We could get really high. I have some cocaine."

"Whoa there," Amber put out her hands.

"It's good stuff, I think. I've been saving it for an occasion. Did you drive? You can leave your car."

"Let's just stick to wine for now."

For the first time her host's enthusiasm dimmed, but only for a moment. Her smile leapt back into action: "You can't say no to food. Hang on."

She brought back from the kitchen a plate of cut vegetables, berries, and dip. They began talking about food and when Amber admitted that she was not much of a cook, Rose was delighted by what she took to be the intimacy of this confession. Amber's secret was safe with her, she said, and gave another short-lived giggle.

A high machinic whine tore into the room and halted the conversation. Just where this sound, like that of a bandsaw, was coming from Amber was unsure: outside maybe, but not distant, or could it be upstairs, behind a closed door?

"What was that?"

"I'm really happy to see you again," Rose said, staring down at her open palms. "Sometimes it comes over me, this freezing cold, starting at my fingers and my feet, freezing them, so they can't move, and then my hands can't move and then my arms and legs, like they're all frosted white and frozen solid and. And it's. So cold."

Amber hesitated, looking back at the staircase going up into darkness, now silent, and then looking at Rose's hands held out as though they and she were indeed frozen.

"Didn't you hear it, that noise?"

"Publishing, that must be very exciting work," Rose said, still looking at her outstretched hands. Slowly she folded them into her lap and went on, now smiling at Amber, "I remember that you were always creative. It must be very rewarding to be able to use your imagination and creativity at work."

Amber tried to explain that her work was mostly in promotion, and only so much creativity was involved, but Rose refilled their glasses and pressed on: "It must be very rewarding. The Shoe Depot is not exactly a dream career. But I've never been a creative person."

The metal shriek sounded again, this time for only a few seconds. Again Rose seemed not to notice, but drank her wine without touching the plate of food.

How lonely, if that's the right word, must I be that I am here, Amber wondered. The warm embrace of the wine was gone. It was past midnight, nearing the babysitter's time. No, only past eleven: that noise had her rattled. Rose Parsomething giggled again.

"The guy I got the cocaine from, you should have seen him."

Amber stood and reached for her purse, but Rose seized it from the floor to her chest as though it were a baby yanked back from a fire.

"It's been great catching up like this."

"We haven't even opened the tequila."

"Hard to believe that I was ever that young. But speaking of young, there's a babysitter waiting."

"Make her wait," rasped Rose. "That's what babysitters are for. We're making a night of it."

"Another time, we'll do that. But I'm afraid I am tired and have to be going."

Rose bared her teeth and said nothing: the two of them

were a tableau, and this thought so unexpectedly angered Amber that a moment later she reached across and pulled the purse sharply to her. I'm not a tableau, her mind's chorus fiercely repeated, I am in motion. She rescued her jacket from the front closet and at the door noticed that Rose had not come to join her, so looked back to say as cheery a good-bye as she might manage.

Rose, unmoved from her seat, was staring at her with convulsive fear.

I am not a tableau.

She gently pulled the door shut behind her.

Parsons. That was it.

III

Late Tuesday morning, right after running some late proofs to the printer, Amber found herself near Rose's neighbourhood, and with no decision on the point let her hands steer the car to the house. She had been rude, there was no way of getting around it, just as there was no way of just letting that lie. Her mind, her mind.

However, this unannounced visit made no sense to her even as she was making it. Surely she would not be home, but at work, though Amber at least understood that she didn't actually want to encounter her. Then what gesture was she making, and for whom? She was at the doorstep and, looking at the bell, recalled how Rose had answered the door so promptly, and in that dress, which might well have been new. She was still looking at the bell. Better not ring. What's the point of ringing? Nobody to.

Rose's father. But there was no nurse's car in the drive. Better not ring. Leave a note?

Saying what, exactly?

Start writing it and it will get written. The distinctive timbre, there, of the platitudinous voice of an ex-husband, always encouraging of nothing in particular. She was not writing; she was leaning over the railing to look inside the window.

But there was nothing to see. The window was criss-crossed with frost.

IV

Normally she threw the local newspaper swathed in advertising straight into the recycling bin, but that Thursday evening she had wanted to scan for some notice about the rumoured school closure. And that was when she saw it. Tableau: unmoving woman reading news article over kitchen counter. I am not, I am, I am a tableau.

But on Monday she was in motion again, driving to the funeral home, circling to find it and circling again to find parking, unwilling to give up this motion. The article said nothing more specific than "an accident." Asking around at work the next day turned up no further details but the school closure announced that morning was in every conversation. "Suddenly." Both father and daughter. "An accident."

Not many people were at the memorial, and Amber's attention immediately fell to a seated woman clasping hands, hers and others, in a sequence. Two caskets were closed; Rose opted to approach the living. To say what?

Start speaking and it will get spoken.

"You must be Rose's sister," Amber said. "I am so very sorry."

A more tired version of Rose's eyes quickly sized her up. The woman nodded and pursed her lips. "Everybody's sorry," she said.

There were no eulogies. For too long Amber examined the flowers and she felt the sister's stare at her back. Another mourner, apparently pleased to provide such information, came up to her and pointed to this or that floral arrangement as she identified the senders in a sucking whisper: Wanda, the Joost family, the nurse, the Shoe Depot, the furnace company where Rose's father had worked for nearly forty years.

"Did he work with tools, machines, that sort of thing?"

"I didn't really know him, myself, but I suppose he must have."

What kind of accident? Amber asked the whisperer with her eyes, but the question somehow never reached her, and she had merely said that there was peace for them now.

Outside the sun was still obliviously shining. And it was not cold at all.

A LONG FLY BALL TO BECAUSE

I do my crosswords upside down. It sounds crazy but bear me out on this. I do the crossword upside down. Now what does that tell you?

What

That's neuroplasticity, that is. I can look into my mind and say to my mind, think differently, and your mind tells your brain. Hence the brain changes.

I'm not clever

You don't have to be clever! I'm not talking about being clever or not being clever, you don't have to be clever, all right!

But it helps, right

Your mind, that is, your mental faculties. You've got to challenge them, haven't you, or what have you got?

Never thought about it like that

Now you're just encouraging him.

Because it's all so precarious. Everything you are, all of what makes you you, what makes the world the world for you, all of it up here.

This is going to give me a headache.

A headache might do you some good. But let me give you

Mighty generous today. Your round, isn't it?

I'll give you an example.

Wait till I have a full glass, do me that sweet mercy.

An example of what?

I'll give you an example, a true story. There's this concert pianist, totally brilliant, IQ off the charts, that kind of phenomenon. Does tours all over the world and speaks several languages fluently.

Probably does his crosswords upside down.

Obviously he was never anywhere near our Andy's level of genius, but this is a true story, all right!

I want to hear the rest of the story, if there is any.

So a certified brilliant musician, his star still rising when he hits forty and what happens, he goes to bed late one night after helping himself to a big slice of pie from the fridge, has a terrible night, tossing and turning. When he wakes up the next morning he is all cheerful but has trouble with words, keeps repeating himself. His wife tries to calm him by taking him to the piano but it's gone, he can't play, it's just like the language, nothing but repeating and going back and forth. And that's the rest of his life, always cheerful, but incoherent, lost.

Whatsis name

What's whose name

You guys sound like

This concert pianist, whatsis name?

Master of the irrelevant, that's you.

Sound like those guys who used to do that old routine, you know

Here I'm trying to sound a cautionary note about the precariousness of our cognitive, our cognitive existences, all right?

The one about the baseball players' names, whatever it was they were called

And I tell you that genius, certified genius can have just a bad night in bed, no reason or warning, and wake up barely able to string a sentence together

What was it, the two of them, you know

And in the face of this daunting, unfathomable mystery of the mind, all this character wants to know

Laurel and Hardy, was it? It might have

Abbott and Costello.

What?

Abbott and

What?

I am beginning to think that what is your favourite word. Even when there's a match on, you're all what, what, what the whole way through.

I said I'm not clever but

There's clever and dumb and bright and guileless and all sorts of categories like all of the silly names you see for paints in a hardware store and none of them tells you anything about colour or about the paint, just like none of those categories tells you about anybody's mind or brain. You're clever or you're not clever one moment doing one thing and the next moment you're something different.

If the next moment you're something different

Look out, he's going well past what

how can you know who you are, if that keeps changing?

Finally a question worth the asking. You may say it comes from an unexpected quarter, still waters running deep and all that, but the rest of you

Ron Ron Ron Ron Runaway!

You might try keeping up with Ronnie here, honestly. And do you know what, I can't answer that question, all right, because nobody can.

The daunting, unfathomable mystery of the

Nobody has figured that one out yet, Ronnie.

Give us your theory, then, for surely you have one.

Andy, we'll all miss you when you finally take the hint. I know what I read, all right, and there are of course theories out there, theories about how we might be only thinking that we're the same person all the time, theories about

If it's as late as I think it is, I have to become pops again and get to the boy's birthday, get glared at by my daughter-in-law. What time is it?

Few minutes before three.

As I feared.

Stolen Kiss, that's the worst name

What

Reverting to form there.

Paint colour. It was one Louisa picked out for a bathroom a couple of years back when we had it done. Stolen Kiss. I put my foot down.

You pick your battles.

I'll have one more, thanks, but I give up on doing all the lifting of the intellectual bar around here. Talk about neuro-plasticity! Andy, it was terrible to see you.

You're just saying that because nobody but me actually

listens to you. And I only listen to you because you don't call me pops and expect me to buy you something every ten minutes.

You're blessed and you don't know it. It's a blessing to have grandkids.

You can say that with a full glass in your hand far from the battle!

Our hearts go with you. Don't they, lads?

Hearts, hearts but not brains

What

Any moment now, isn't that right, we'll all be somebody else

That's right

So best wishes but no promises.

Fair enough.

Fair enough for now, you mean.

Is that what I mean? I wondered.

We all did. Isn't that right?

A PEOPLE'S HISTORY

It began, as you might suppose, as a bit of a lark, and like most larks, this one was a pulled punch against loneliness. The first gatherings, with no better title or description, took place in the most modest hotels to offer something like a banquet space, usually somewhere on the edge of cities like Tulsa, Cincinnati, Winnipeg. One evening, goofy and awkward, made up of nametags and beer and a couple of guitars, was followed the next year by another, this time with a small band, all of them members, and by the third year there was enough of a tradition to balance the goofy with the awkward and introduce formality. For application purposes, only birth certificates were acceptable, and some codes of conduct were formulated after an unfortunate scene at the Syracuse gathering, and the complaints that arose from it: two members, Danny Kaye and Isaac Newton, started a fistfight that caused thousands of dollars of damage to a ballroom. Gradually, as the founders passed on their organizational offices to new generations, though the codes of conduct were retained and refined, any legal identification was deemed qualification enough, which meant that "changers," as they were called, were admitted.

This did not settle the matter for the membership, and the resentment smoldered. When Burt Reynolds, known to be opposed to the inclusion of "changers," was elected secretary, to the surprise of the other elected officers, he helped put forward and support motions designed to limit or discourage the participation of "changers." His efforts spawned a resistance movement, led by Jeanne d'Arc and Muhammad Ali, a married couple from Florida. They pointedly asked whether the society was nothing more than a matter of flukes and coincidences, or whether it might not, as they believed, point to some deeper commitment to heroism and identification with heroes. Eventually they went further, writing in a newsletter edited by the fastidiously impartial Diana Ross, that if the latter were the case, "changers" were in effect more invested than "birthers." The notoriously raucous convention in Walla Walla saw the election of Frank Zappa, militant "changer," as president, and his address stunned the crowd with the suggestion that future membership rules might be loosened yet further to admit those with the famous names of *fictional* people. It is generally believed that this event triggered the break-up of the d'Arc-Ali marriage, since she supported Zappa and he did not, as well as the lonely suicide of Roger Moore, Zappa's most moderate opponent in the election, and the earliest surreptitious investigations of the society by federal intelligence officers.

The following summer a group of "birthers" organized their own private "retreat" in a resort in Vermont. It was later discovered that, of the thirty-three in attendance, only twenty were actually "birthers"; the rest were either "changers" with fake birth certificates or federal investigators — including Gladys Knight, who exposed the frauds when she herself quit the agency and legally changed her name. A plot was hatched to "remove" Zappa, though it was never entirely clear whether violence was to be used. At any rate, Knight's revelations strengthened the resolve of the "changers," and not only was Zappa re-elected for a subsequent term, fellow "changers" Cher and John Wilkes Booth were elected as vice-president and treasurer, respectively. This brought about the controversial consultations with Baron Samedi, a man who represented a group of "fictionals" lobbying for admission to the society. These talks took place at a meeting of the executive in a hotel in Newark. At the conclusion of that weekend's first session, Zappa retired to his room, from which he was taken by unknown persons. An unsigned note left behind announced that any deal with the "fictionals" would mean the death of the president, as would any attempt to contact law enforcement.

At the time it was believed that a faction of "birthers" equally opposed to both "changers" and "fictionals" were responsible, but the true culprits were "changers" opposed to "fictionals." This group was led by Akhenaton, a somewhat shadowy figure who seldom appeared at society gatherings but was a vociferous correspondent in the newsletter's pages. Akhenaton was emphatic about the society's allegiance, as he put it, with history: it would not do to allow the names of people who never existed the same legitimacy as the names of those who did and who were thus remembered, allowed to live yet in the present. Before Akhenaton's role was made known, however, a number of "birthers" known to be opposed to the talks with Baron Samedi, fell victim to misplaced retaliations: Thomas Edison was beaten into a coma as he walked home one night from the laundromat; Cesar Romero was poisoned at his favourite tavern; Dorothy L. Sayers and an unnamed friend died in a suspicious boating accident near Cape Cod.

The attendance numbers at the following convention, held in Fort Wayne, were a record high, as were the number of federal investigators, drawn by the unsolved attacks on Edison, Romero, and Sayers. During the proceedings, Yuri Gagarin, a "changer," demanded to know why the president was not there. Unsatisfactory answers from Cher sparked a call for a new election, which society by-laws permitted. The results found "birther" Ken Holcombe president by a narrow margin. Cher was re-elected vice president by an even slimmer difference of votes, but John Wilkes Booth was replaced by "changer" Marie Tussaud, while a new Roger Moore became secretary. After the customary banquet, a letter was delivered to Holcombe: it implied that Zappa was dead, and that any further discussions with Baron Samedi and his people would have similar consequences.

The federal investigators who, like Gladys Knight before them, joined the ranks of the "changers" after being so impressed by their time at the convention, helped the executive members determine the whereabouts of Akhenaton, though it took some time, and a couple of wrongly identified apartment buildings were destroyed by fires. Akhenaton's ravings were not included in the subsequent newsletter. He hid himself in the Bahamas, where a waiter named George

Mallory reported having found and dispatched him with a length of piano wire. This news was quickly followed by that of Mallory's own death, no doubt at the hands of Akhenaton's fellow "allies of history."

Sensing an opportunity, Baron Samedi contacted the society executive to point out that these renegade "allies of history" would prove destructive to the society as a whole, pitting "birther" against "changer" and vice-versa, operating outside the accepted chain of command within the society. Allowing the "fictionals" admission to the society would, he wrote, strengthen the support for the executive considerably, and these many and eager new members could be deployed to bring to heel any of Akhenaton's unrepentant "allies." Tussaud's proposal that membership fees for "fictionals" be twice that of other members achieved an otherwise elusive consensus.

Almost immediately membership quadrupled. This surge necessitated the appointment of regional directors and, accordingly, plans for regional conventions to complement the annual general meeting. Even more federal investigators left the deeply perplexed agency to join the society, as did a governor from the midwest. Akhenaton's right-hand man, Henry Mancini, was drowned in a kiddie pool in his backyard the very day that Baron Samedi signed his own membership card. Yet at the moment of his triumph, Samedi was faced with serious questions about his status in the society: why was he claiming to be a "fictional," when many, among them the ambitious young Ida Bauer, suggested that he was properly a "changer." These questions were loaded: Samedi had to be sure, on the one hand, not to offend those in the society who might believe that his namesake had some factual existence and, on the other, not to appear sympathetic to the very "allies of history" against whom he had mobilized the new membership. The executive coolly offered Samedi no assistance in this regard, and Bauer became president in the next election at Spartanburg. She and her vice president, Frodo Baggins, almost certainly masterminded the bloody killings of Samedi, Lionel Ritchie, Betty Boop, and Friar Tuck. But when the assassination of John Travolta, the director of the East Coast who was thought to be siphoning society funds, was bungled, Speedy Gonzales was arrested and made a deal to turn state's witness against the society. Thanks to the influence of well-placed members, media reports of the case tended to ridicule the whole thing, and drew attention to the declining ranks of federal investigators to suggest the desperate need for relevance. Other suggestions were thrown into the public arena: that the real John Travolta, the actor, had been the intended target; that Speedy Gonzales was insane, as his change of name suggested; that the "attack" was nothing more than a stunt for a forthcoming film.

As Bauer sought ways to extend her tenure as president beyond the term allowed by society rules, she took note of some of the competitors and threats around her, but not all. She was keenly aware, for instance, of the inordinate number of Roger Moores in the society, and had figured out that they were, as a group, quietly dedicated to avenging the sad death of the society's first Roger Moore years before, and were thus opposed to any changes to the society's constitution since that time, though they did not declare it, but rather bided their time. Bauer also knew that Travolta, though he had kept faith with the society, would not forget, and Benjamin Spock, the regional director of the Southwest, repeatedly and openly challenged Bauer's decisions and her fitness for the presidency. However, she did not anticipate the open letter, circulated at the Elizabethtown convention, allegedly written by Akhenaton.

The question of whether this was the same Akhenaton as the originator of the "allies of history," not in fact killed by George Mallory, dominated the convention. Spock, a "birther," seized the chance to denounce Bauer, citing the troubles caused by "fictionals" such as Gonzales, the unpopular Baggins, and Holly Golightly, a dominatrix who had starred in a documentary in which she hinted perhaps a little too much about the society. Inevitably, a snap election was called, in which over three dozen candidates were nominated for president, including Spock, Travolta, and four Roger Moores. A furious Bauer attacked Spock in his hotel room and blinded him before Horatio Nelson, his bodyguard, killed her, an act which began a night of reprisals. By the next day's vote, only ten candidates were still standing for the office. Shirley Temple, a "birther" from the earliest days of the society, won. Though she promised a campaign aimed at addressing differences in a more peaceful manner, the new vice president, Thomas Tank Engine, poured scorn and abuse on the "allies of history" and their open letter.

When Engine's body was fished out of a Detroit sewer less than a month later, civil war erupted. The chief players were members from the East Coast who took their cues from blind Benjamin Spock, rabid "fictionals" who had supported Thomas Tank Engine and now followed Pallas Athena, and two factions of the "allies of history," one presumably led by Akhenaton, and the other, unwilling to recognize even "changers," led by Howard Cosell and tacitly supported by the Roger Moores. Political lobbyists made up of or employed by the latter two groups worked hard to pass legislation in several states forbidding people from changing their names to those of trademark characters, and they enjoyed the backing of a number of large corporations who otherwise had little or no affiliation with the society. This was made somewhat easier by the number of judges and civil servants who belonged to the society, but the "changers," and especially those whose adopted names were those of people whose historical authenticity might be challenged, had strong concerns about how any such legislation might be used against them. At a press conference in Chicago, a number of Akhenaton-run politicians were gunned down by HAL 9000 and Big Ethel. When police cornered the killers, they detonated a bomb that destroyed most of three city blocks.

The society was thereafter named an illegal organization by the President of the United States. That president's name some of you, perhaps, may remember.

HANGING OFFENCES

Herpes, the internet said.

Painful genital sores, bleed easily, wash hands carefully, recurrent outbreaks, no cure, unfair, unfair.

Unfair too because the guy who has infected her, the guy who had looked briefly up from her belly to avow that the coldsore below his lip was just a coldsore, this was just a guy she was seeing for a while, just a while, nothing serious. She texted him and, by way of telling him that she was done with him, told him to get himself checked, and his reply was: *Thanks, I will. Really.*

And do you know who had introduced them?

The internet.

Fine.

Of course she could manage a full day of hanging a new show. It's fine that the artist's lengthy instructions are unclear and giving her a headache. It's fine that Brooke was in her most voluble mode and wanted to talk about her friend's upcoming wedding, her other friend's legal troubles, and her creepy neighbour, the one who keeps offering to trim her hedge. All of that was fine because it kept her focus away from the two computers in the gallery and what else the internet might have to say, so she read the artist's instructions over and over, sometimes aloud, and she enthused about the wedding and sympathized with the litigation and expressed shock at the trim-hedging offers, all in the right order.

It was raining lightly when she cycled home and the wires high above her hummed. She scowled at them, conductors of electricity and purveyors of the internet.

When she got home, the internet reminded her that there were antiviral drugs available. The rain stopped but the moon kept itself hidden behind ambiguous clouds. What was the point of the moon? Spying, spied upon rock, secretly without secrets of its own.

She was awakened by a dream of having herpes. She was on some sort of gameshow and somehow, to her horror, won it as a prize. The applause of the crowd was rain: it was raining again, this time with conviction.

She considered going to see her therapist, but Felicity was really into this role-playing strategy lately, and just the phrase conjured up all sorts of discouragement. For all she knew this month, all given to role-playing, was pirate month, so it would be all *what be grieving ye, ye scurvy dog* and she didn't need that just now. She opened up her laptop and gulped down coffee. In an email sent to all of her friends and contacts, she announced that she was going offline for the foreseeable future. Within moments she had four messages commending her for this decision; none of them asked why.

A block from home she got a puncture, walked the bike

back, fixed it, got to the gallery twenty-some minutes late, made apologetic sounds to Brooke, sat down at her desk to scan the morning's agenda when she noticed, slowly so weirdly slowly, that the pictures she had carefully yesterday carefully were now hung in a completely different order. For a while she semi-surreptitiously eyed Brooke, as much watchful for any sign as vaguely hoping to compel a confession or explanation. She ostentatiously reviewed the printed pages of the artist's instructions, and then slowly walked to the wall of pictures.

Turning to Brooke at last, still not sure what she was about to say, she discovered her crying. The information could only be extracted between thick, choking sobs: her friend, her friend who was getting married next month, she had just uninvited her from the wedding, just like that. By email.

Painful genital sores.

Shoulder set to comforting all morning, and though Brooke refused to go home for the afternoon, agreed to take a longer lunch. Thanks, I will. The moment she was out the door, the artist's instructions were back in her hand and she advanced on the pictures.

What she had arranged yesterday looked like this:

| 1 | 3 | 5 | 7 | 9 | 12 | 14 | 16 | 18 | 20 | |
| 2 | 4 | 6 | 8 | 10 | 11 | 13 | 15 | 17 | 19 | 21 |

And now it looked like this:

| 9 | 20 | 8 | 1 | 19 | 14 | 15 | 3 | 21 | 18 | 5 |
| 10 | 7 | 13 | 2 | 16 | 17 | 4 | 11 | 12 | 6 | |

Her lips were moving as she worked: *Strange, ay, are the things you find far from land.*

Thanks very much.

She managed to finish just before Brooke returned. Brooke fiercely emoted vulnerability and neediness for the rest of the afternoon.

Fine.

The next night was the opening. The artist would be present. She was probably going to turn out to be a jerk.

The next morning she scolded her hand and withdrew it from the laptop, to which it had leapt. She made her coffee as strong as she could handle, in part because she had somehow emptied a bottle of wine the night before, watching a documentary about the intelligence of crows, all the while suspecting it was really about something else. There was also the opening: that would require a little more, what, strength maybe, endurance, something.

A small victory in arriving at the gallery early, even before Brooke, who always seemed to be there, dissolved when she found:

14   15   15   21   20   2   18   5   1   11   19
15   15   15   15   15   15   15   15   15   15

The repeated images, the duplicate pictures, stared back at her, but were they defiant, amused, what? And what was she? Pirate month still had a week and a half to go.

At eleven o'clock she called Brooke at home, but no answer. She had not touched the pictures. She wanted to, she wanted to take them all down, or maybe turn them around, to see the uniform, featureless backs of all of them, in a way that the order in which they were hung wouldn't matter. She didn't want to, there was no way she was going to go through all that again, she was not going to move from her desk, she was not even going to look at the pictures.

What were the pictures of?

What kind of question is that? And besides, she wasn't looking at them.

Not really.

She went to the toilet and turned her suppressed glare on her groin. For a moment she wondered if there was a pattern there, an order. But that's the opposite of order, she nearly said aloud. The opening was to start in just over three hours. The moon, wherever it was, could go fuck itself.

When she came out of the bathroom, after torturing her hands with the most scalding water she could summon, she said, really aloud, Fine, looking at the wall with its single picture:

15

It was massive: this single picture had swallowed up all the others, taken over the whole wall. She didn't move.

At some point the phone started ringing.

But then the opening: pouring wine, trying to say hello to everyone, excuses for Brooke who couldn't be here, all as though she were doing all of it without her doing any of it, and in front of her was the artist, who was apologizing for something, none of the recognizable jerk traits perceptible, even Felicity was there, relaxed and very much ashore, enthusing about a show with just one picture, but it feels like so many pictures doesn't it, and when she answered, maybe a couple of dozen, not even the artist seemed to notice, and it was all so immediate, so living and change and awkward and how did this happen.

Somebody, not the internet, was asking if she would have another glass.

She said, but only so carefully, Thanks, I will.

AGAINST TYPE

The murderer of the casting director has to be right-handed. His hair should be dark blonde, cut short and kept with no fuss, and his eyes bright and watchful. Not exceptionally tall, though slightly taller than his victim, and only approaching handsome at quiet, unexpected moments, without aware-ness of it. Strong but not obviously so: no bulk of any kind, but an implied solidity. Strong hands. He should brush the back of his neck when he stands up. Good posture. The trace of an accent now and then in his speech, maybe Dutch, though he does not generally speak more than he needs to, and only uses one word wrongly, in as much as he uses it too often without purpose: "essentially," as in such phrases as "I am essentially a relaxed personality" or "I like to know what you think this role, this character is essentially about." Chuckles warmly and, it seems, genuinely, rather than laughs. Must wear no jewellery of any kind. His eyes must flicker around a room when he enters it, as though getting his bearings, and this tendency may grow more pronounced, even more frantic, as he returns again and again to offices such as that of this casting director. His smile, never over-

done, with only the slightest flash of teeth, is always acti-
vated when he enters these rooms: only the eyes' perhaps
involuntary tour of the room changes, shows how uncertain and agitated he is becoming, how ravaged by each new
rejection, how desperate in a way not even fully known to
himself, but these things are only barely visible. Even less
visible is the anger, the rage deep within him, an animal
hurling itself against the ribs that cage it, watching for an
opening, a chance to lash out at everything and anything
that may have trapped it. Everything, everything depends
on his getting this part.

HER·FEET

She doesn't care for us, said Left.

Right did not answer, so Left elaborated: She doesn't like us. She is ashamed of us.

What good will come of talking about it, Right, the more Gallic of the two, answered wearily.

Uncovered by the bedsheet, their ankles communed gently in earliest morning. Just as they may fall asleep after resting in position, so too do they wake on their own, for reasons of which even they may not be certain.

It bothers you, too. You know it does.

Right sighed. Those who have heard feet sigh know what a profound melancholy is shared in hearing it. But the foot rallied, after a moment, and said, She has never abused us. Physically, I mean.

You enjoy all of those shoes she chooses to wear, Left tartly replied.

Well, look. Some of those shoes are lovely, but that's not the point. We can have aesthetic differences but those are hardly substantial grievances. And yes, we carry everything, we are pressed and beaten by the earth, but that's the job description, isn't it? We're not lungs or eyelids or teeth or, or anything else! We have to do what we have to do and there's no good to be had in complaining about it. And we have some bad days. Terrible days. And some of the shoes are wretched. But that's not the point!

This was the longest speech that Right had made in many months, and it gave them both pause. Left wondered whether the ears were listening, and of course they were, for that's all that ears do: they greedily, indiscriminately absorb sounds, but just as a glutton does not truly savour food, the ears — even these ears, which when nibbled would dispatch thrilling shrieks all along the nerves and have the whole skin horripilate — consumed and left collation and assessment to the brain, which at this time was by its custom immersed in trifles and obscenities and not available for comment. For their part, the ears did not care.

Left tried another approach: So you're content.

I didn't say —

Or, Left continued, there's nothing to be done. Which one is it?

You really want to talk about this?

You don't? countered Left. I know you're unhappy. You know that she doesn't like us.

It would be nice if she didn't speak so badly about us.

She doesn't even keep it to herself!

The neck, which might not have been fully awake, chuckled to itself.

Through the open window came the voices of the workmen on the roof of the building opposite, calling to each other with the usual workday greetings and complaints, banging about and turning on a radio that gave voice to music from people who were decades older at this moment than they were when they had recorded this music, or even now dead, their arms and kidneys and eyes not awake and not conversing, not singing and not asleep but utterly inoperative, sounds drawn into her ears, living ears that did not speak but passed along to the brain, which would have to work through all of this material eventually, awake or otherwise.

If we were to become detached —

Free from her?

It would have to be a cut —

Something sharp.

Something sharp. Then we'd be free.

It would have to be quick, Left's voice quavered a little.

Something like, like an industrial accident.

Neither of them had ever set itself upon a factory floor. Left could not help thinking of a bottling plant, or at least what Left supposed a bottling plant must look like, with rows of bottles being filled and capped and shoved along by other bottles waiting to be filled and capped and shoved along, and could not envisage how such mechanisms would allow for a swift, liberating amputation.

I don't know, I don't know.

Merveilleux, said Right. You don't know. You started this conversation.

We have to do something. We're agreed on that much, aren't we?

Merveilleux, Right said again. Right was sullenly remembering the recent occasions that Left had gotten in the way while walking.

Perhaps the hands would help us, said Left. We could ask the hands to help us!

Left correctly interpreted Right's silence to mean that the hands would not help anyone, the hands were only in it for themselves, the hands could not be trusted. Left had never mentioned this to Right, but Left had a bit of a thing for hands.

You're a poor judge when it comes to hands, said Right. You've always had a bit of a thing for them.

Left, shocked, did not know what to say.

Voices from the past carried by the radio to the ears asked whether you wanna dance under the moonlight, squeeze me baby all through the night, oh baby, do you wanna dance?

The bladder began to rouse itself. The bladder was never fully awake, and never fully asleep, or at any rate it seemed to dislike either extreme.

We're going to start work any minute, Right observed.

Recognizing this unnecessary observation as an attempt to be friendly, Left eventually answered, Yes.

Do you do you do you do you wanna dance?

It's not their best song, Left said.

I didn't mean anything bad about, about your thing for hands. Right gave a short cough, which the ears gulped down. You know, I've noticed it, that's all.

Well, said Left.

Whatever you're into, Right continued. Whatever makes you happy.

Her hands prefer not to touch us.

I never gave it much —

Think about it now.

The bladder was muttering in its ancient language.

Maybe this whole discussion of escape from her is crazy. Maybe we should consider some kind of job action. You know, refuse to work until we get more respect.

It's worth a try.

You think so?

I do, yes.

All right.

And you know what else?

I'm all ears, said Right. To borrow an expression.

Let's hold out for a specific concession. I'm thinking a holiday. A holiday for us.

It's been a long time since we went dancing.

A night of dancing.

Go bigger. A night of dancing somewhere fantastic.

Switzerland. A night of dancing in Switzerland.

Then the universe stretched and stretched. The nose was suddenly drunk and the eyes resumed their harrumphing debate on everything and anything. The brain was waking. She.

A night of dancing in Switzerland!

Fair and just demands.

She was going to get up, hair and arms and waist were moving, she was getting up.

And bathing in a river. Let's demand that, too.

In Switzerland.

Yes, said Right.

I can see it now, said Left.

SAFETY

The man who sold me the gun told me it would work. All day yesterday I looked for him and asked around for him and could not find him. Even if the money cannot be returned all that is needed is a better one or else show me what I am doing wrong. I looked for him and I could not find him. What am I going to tell the landlady?

THE ODDS

A few years ago a survey was taken of all applicants for marriage licences in one of the States, I forget which one; Texas, it might have been. The applicants were to answer a pair of interesting questions. The first, a question of fact, asked what was the divorce rate, in percentage form, in the state, the answer to which was fifty percent, the average rate not just of the state but of the nation as a whole. All of the applicants got this question right. The second question asked: what is the likelihood, in percentage form, that your marriage, the marriage for which you are now applying for a state licence, will end in divorce? Again, the answers were unanimous. All of the applicants answered: zero.

It is not difficult to see either the ardour or the determination, whichever it may have been, if those two can be distinguished from one another, behind the conviction that constitutes that second answer, utterly absurd and unrealistic as it is in the face of the answer to the first question. Passion disregards logic, or rather, it has a logic all of its own, a pathology really, that surpasses all other forms of reasoning as easily as you step over the hard labour of hundreds of ants far beneath your notice.

Or perhaps some of the applicants thought it was a trick question: if they answered it incorrectly, which is to say honestly and plausibly, their application might be denied on the grounds that they weren't serious about matrimonial commitment. This possibility, though it probably never occurs to the kind of people who devise these questionnaires and tabulate the responses, for whatever harmless end, takes purchase in the imagination and grows there. Ought one to sympathize with such people, hesitating before the altar as it were, or ought one to find them ridiculous? And if both, which response in which measure? Are marriages, or even human relationships in general, a matter of probabilities, or are they based on playing against the odds, ignoring the odds?

I mentioned this survey to a friend of mine recently, and because he is something of a public figure, I will omit his name here. Also because he is a something of a public figure, when the two of us meet for drinks some place, usually a quiet bar just off the beaten track, we take the opportunity to unwind and after the first round he allows himself some candid admissions in conversation. He is near retirement but not one for woolgathering. Though his face is lined and his hair mostly grey, he remains a handsome man. But perhaps his most striking feature is his sincerity, in evidence at all times, even when he is at his most reserved, as he wasn't on this occasion when I told him about the survey. It is so complete an aura of sincerity that he projects that it is impossible to doubt it, and yet it is equally impossible not to feel that such doubts are without foundation, are base and undeserved.

As he listened to me tell him about the survey, and I saw his smile broaden, I suddenly found myself thinking of another evening of our drinking together, though not alone, years before. At that time my friend was in the early days of what was, in my view, probably an ill-advised affair. I say "ill-advised" not as any kind of moral judgment, not at all, but simply as a matter of pragmatism, because the woman in question lived in the same small city that my friend and his wife did, and they all knew each other, and it is probably wisest, in my inexpert opinion, to keep one's affairs at a somewhat greater remove, as it were. And I say "early days" as a kind of guess, because I'm naturally not sure at exactly what date and time the two of them officially commenced the affair, however that might be measured; and for that matter I might as well add that I can't be entirely sure that there was an affair, because I have no certain knowledge of it, and he has never told me of it. The woman in question, whose name has to be omitted for the same reason given earlier, had been openly smitten for quite a while and regularly managed to turn up at parties and events where he might be, and she liked to repeat things he had said, sometimes weeks before, not just crediting him but inevitably providing a careful set-up to the story, to present his words in the best possible light. She knew his favourite music and it was her favourite music.

We were, a large group of us, at a restaurant patio one midsummer evening, following a ceremony of some sort, I forget exactly what it was about, but my friend had given a little speech at it, the sort of thing he always did with no small charm, even if he sometimes privately complained to me afterwards how little he enjoyed making those kinds of speeches. It was a late dinner and the tables pushed together were crowded with drinks. There was a lively discussion about what was going on in Greece and eventually Kittredge got up and did his usual imitation of a gorilla; all in all a fairly ordinary night of its kind, a night of drink and talk and laughter and tedious antics. And then the waitress brought the bills, always a sticky business with such a large group and so many different orders, and this waitress brought a single bill to my friend and this woman with whom he had not quite yet, I think, begun an affair, though many signs were pointing in that direction. It must be said that my friend was never one to give trouble to waitresses, unless it was in the kinds of special requests he sometimes liked to make, always in a soothing, deferential tone, about this dish or that drink. I mean that he was never rude or irritable, never trouble as a customer, but when this waitress brought this single bill for the both of them, his eyes opened wide, needlessly wide, to show how he was momentarily overcome with confusion, and when his eyes resumed their customary aspect and the woman with whom he had been sharing a generous dish of oysters had stepped off to the toilet, he looked at me and asked, "Why do they assume that we are together?"

Often with my friend, this maker of speeches, it took me a moment or two to see whether these kinds of questions were rhetorical, or whether he actually expected an answer. This was apparently of the latter category, for he was look-ing expectantly at me. "Well," I answered, "you sat next to one another and shared the same order, you shared the oysters. It seems logical to assume that you would be sharing the expense." He held his palms to the sky. He lowered his voice only slightly and said to me and those closest to him at the table, "This happens all the time. People assume that we're together." So completely baffled by this situation did he seem that it was impossible to know how genuine the bafflement was; in fact, it seemed so overdone that one felt uncomfortable even doubting how genuine it might be. This was a key part of that charm I mentioned, part of his indisputable ability to win over audiences when making speeches or simply when dealing with waitresses in restaurants.

His wife, I need hardly say, was not among the company that night. She did not, in the years I knew her, much care for parties or crowds. She was a sculptor and preferred the contemplation of stone to chattering groups. Her contributions to any conversation were firm but slight. "That's how she is," my friend would say, sometimes with a shrug that said, "and I would not have it any other way," or in other company and in other situations with a quick downward look that said, "so you see what I have to deal with." Did she once think or say that there was zero percent chance of her marriage coming to an end?

It must have been anticipation of the way that my friend would respond to my telling him about the survey that made me suddenly think of that earlier evening when he asked, with all of that sincerity that seemed too much, "Why do they assume that we're together?" Maybe I expected to see those wide, wide eyes again, that incredulity that was so hard to believe but, seen, had to be believed. This was not what happened. Instead, he chuckled, but in that chuckle

I thought I recognized a note of some discomfort or irritation. Didn't he think that was interesting, that universally given pair of contradictory answers? He answered slowly: "I wonder what were the ages of those applicants, though perhaps it doesn't matter. Still, it might be interesting to know. We would like to think we get wiser as we age." He finished his drink: he was always showy with his drinks, with what he ordered and how he savoured them. "Are you telling me this because you are thinking of getting married, or because" — and here he named the woman with whom he had had the affair years ago, the affair that had, I assumed, turned out to be ill-advised, not that I or anyone I knew had ever "advised" him about it — "married only a month after my divorce?"

I said I did not know she had married anybody. "She went and married Kittredge. In October. They moved to Vancouver." I had in fact heard something to this effect some time ago but had forgotten it; probably I dismissed it from serious thought, because she had revered my friend. "Revered" is the only word for it, the way she used to repeat his phrases, and it was hard to think how she could possibly transfer such intense feelings to somebody else. And I may have dismissed the notion because Kittredge was a buffoon, always had been, a man whose talents and sophistication were summed up all too well in his incessant gorilla imitations. He was always knocking over other people's drinks with his swinging arms, and always expecting to be forgiven for it just as he was forgiven for being a buffoon, always accepting the forgiveness as his due for being a buffoon. I tried to imagine the two of them, her and this gorilla impersonator, exchanging vows and could not.

A new round of drinks was brought and my friend commended the waitress on something or other: her resemblance to some obscure film star that she would have to look up later, or it might have been her knowledge of malts. I watched this flirtatious scene, with all of its sincerity, play out while I waited to ask my friend, once I determined a decent way to do so, about the affair that we had never discussed, but which he seemed to be tacitly acknowledging by mentioning, without prompting, this marriage to Kittredge, specifically in relation to his own divorce. I drank and watched. The waitress laughed at what my friend was saying, and I imagined him saying to me, "This happens all the time. People assume that we're together." And I wanted to say, "But there are reasons people make assumptions, even if the assumptions aren't true, or were never true." And I wanted to say, "But we're not talking about 'people,' some abstract category, but friends, people whom we trust and with whom we share confidences. The people whose thoughts about us matter to us." I did not say these things, of course, but drank and watched.

When the waitress did finally turn from the table, my friend gave me a strange look. "I think you may have frightened her." What did he mean? I set down my drink, suddenly empty, in a way that was intended to convey amused confusion. "You were talking to yourself, saying things about what isn't true, or what friends you can trust. Something like that, you weren't exactly clear. Downing that last drink isn't going to help matters. I think I had better get you home." We stood up, his hand gently on my shoulder, in case I needed it. "We have found your limit," he laughed, and added: "Any minute now you'll start swinging your arms and acting like a gorilla."

We walked home and joked about how old we had become, old bachelors unable to handle their drink. It was not very late: there were people still in the streets, going from place to place, another fairly ordinary night of people living their lives that only they themselves know. When I think of the people in Texas, or wherever it was, those people applying for marriage licences who found themselves faced with those two questions of percentages, and who became suspicious of those questions, thinking that honest and knowing answers might threaten their chances of being given the licence, I imagine them with eyes opened very wide, shocked, genuinely shocked or too shocked for it to be genuine, I don't know.

PHILOSOPHY

Imagine Martin Heidegger as your skiing instructor!
   That's what he did, for a while, professionally or whatever.
   He really did that.
   Must have been in case, you know, the philosophy didn't
pan out.
   Just imagine!

WHERE CAN I GO WITHOUT YOU?

This is the story of how I saved my friend Roy.

My friend Roy is a city bus driver, an excellent city bus driver. I often ride his bus not because there is any destination along his route that interests me but because he is such an excellent bus driver. His left turns are frankly inspiring. And he is far and away the most patient of all of the city bus drivers.

One day, the eve of the birthday of Peggy Lee, Roy was not on his route. With some dismay I asked the driver where Roy was. This driver made a number of poor left turns. He told me that Roy was unwell, but no details were forthcoming. His lip movements were difficult to read because he had a beard, of the unkempt variety.

So the next day when I ascertained that Roy was still not on his route, I went to Roy's house. It took me just three guesses from the half a block or so I had figured his house must be in. His sister answered the door, and when I introduced myself, she seemed pleased to meet me and said that she had heard about me from Roy. Her hair was long and made me think of dripping caramel and I asked her whether by any chance she liked caramel and she said yes, sometimes. It was a very interesting conversation but the issue at hand concerned the whereabouts and well-being of Roy. Roy's sister's voice sounded very tired when she told me that Roy had fallen into some sort of coma; it had a technical name but she could no longer think of it and I judged it prudent not to cross-examine. It, this coma with the forgotten technical name, had happened very suddenly and no one had yet determined what had triggered it, the coma with the forgotten technical name. She told me the name of the hospital and his room number and said that it was sweet of me to visit. Caramel is also sweet but I drew no conclusions from this coincidence. After all, it is not for nothing that my advisors repeatedly cautioned me against my habit of drawing unwarranted conclusions, *however well intentioned they might be.*

I proceeded to the hospital and en route exchanged a few friendly words with the driver of bus number eighty-three, which goes past the hospital. His name is Ian and it is interesting that both he and Roy, both bus drivers, have just three letters in their names, but it is doubtful that this connection goes much further than that, since I have encountered other bus drivers with five or six or seven or even more letters in their first name. Still, it is interesting. Ian said that he was very sorry to hear about Roy's coma.

The hospital, which is one of the precisely six hospitals in which I have set foot, feels needlessly crowded and the signs employ mysterious terminology. Finding Roy's room took me longer than expected because of the number of people from whom I had to seek directions. Not all of them spoke clearly. It is very important to speak clearly.

It is always important to speak clearly.

Roy was without visitors when I found his room. Anyone who found him lying there, in that narrow bed and that ghost light, would hardly know that he was a city bus driver, let alone an excellent bus driver, but that he was a good man, surely that would be plain enough, even as he was. That ghost light would not flatter anyone but somehow it took nothing away from him, and maybe even somehow highlighted his essence.

I sat in a chair beside his bed and said it was good to see him. I observed no response and told him that I would just keep talking and that he could join in the conversation at any time. After all, being in a coma frees a person from some of the usual social obligations, and no one could reasonably say that a person in a coma was being rude by not answering everything said to him or her. I told him about the substitute driver on his route, the one with the beard, and about my adventures on bus number eighty-three with Ian. No response. I told him about the weather, both today's and the forecast for the next five days. No response. I told him what a genuine pleasure it was to meet his sister, what a very pleasant person she was, how comfortable I had been conversing with her and she apparently with me. No response. This would not, simply would not dampen my resolve.

"Here's something you might not know," I said to Roy. "Today is the birthday of none other than Peggy Lee. It's also the birthday of John Wayne and Miles Davis and probably many other people but the one I celebrate is Peggy Lee. She was a songwriter as well as a singer. Not a lot of people know that."

Just then a man came into the room. At first I supposed he was a doctor, because he had a businesslike manner to him and he was carrying a clipboard, but almost immediately I could see that he was not a doctor. There was nothing of the doctor about him. I have met thirty-eight doctors and he had nothing like the manner or even the posture of any of them. What's more he did not appear to blink, not even once, which is pretty singular, for a doctor or anyone else. He took a few steps into the room and hesitated, looking at me with his head cocked slightly to one side.

"Peggy Lee," he said, as though he were gurgling some thick liquid as he spoke.

My advisors have offered many good and useful suggestions for interacting with people generally. Some of these suggestions have had to do with detecting tone, or where to put one's hands, or avoiding confusion by speaking clearly. None of them seemed all that applicable in this situation.

"It's her birthday," I said, as clearly as I could manage. "Today."

He turned for a moment to look along Roy in his bed, and then returned his head to its cocked position, looking at me as if with some interest. Again he gurgled, even more slowly this time, "Peggy Lee."

I explained that Roy was indisposed, in a coma no less, a coma with a technical name, which the nurse with the Scottish brogue down the hall would undoubtedly know. I expressed admiration for the hospital, one of six that I myself had been in, and the certainty that all would be well for Roy while in the care of its extremely capable and patient staff. I admitted that the signs could be done better but that point hardly reflected on the medical services available in the facility. All of the time that I was speaking I tried to keep my hands under control but frankly there was something unnerving about this visitor.

His head cocked to the other shoulder at precisely the same angle and his mouth hung open. He lifted the clipboard to his face and only then, when the clipboard had achieved that height and rested there a moment, turned his eyes to it. They did not narrow but stared, still unblinking, very unlike a doctor.

For reasons that remain entirely obscure to me at this moment what should come to my mind but the thought of Mrs. Mantel. There she was vivid in my mind though I had not thought of her in years, this woman who had taken me fishing a number of times one summer when I was a boy and almost never spoke a word. She baited the hook for me every time because I could not and she smiled so lovely while she did it because she always smiled at me and never grew frustrated or cross. Our first time in the boat she winked and said that really I had been the one to catch the big one of the four we brought back and that I deserved all of the credit, and then she could tell something was wrong but she did not grow cross. It would be better, I explained, if we returned them all four to the lake, and if anybody asked we could tell them the fish were not biting at all, and she smiled, she smiled. And every time after that the fish were not biting at all and she showed me how to wink and she would wink back. Mrs. Mantel taught me how to wink and to fish and to be in a boat and many other things that summer, but then we moved again and I never saw her again.

When the thought of Mrs. Mantel dissipated I found that the unblinking man had advanced into the room and was between me and Roy, staring down at him. I stood up from the chair. He seemed to be taller than I had judged.

"I said she wrote songs," I said in a suddenly louder voice. "Song lyrics, Peggy Lee wrote those, and I was telling my friend Roy here that not many people know that." When the man did not move, I said, "I wonder whether you can name even one song written by Peggy Lee."

He turned around, in that slow but deliberate way of all his movements, and gave his gray stare to me.

"Name one," I said.

My advisors, every single one of them, caution always against confrontation. And here I was, speaking very clearly but in what would generally be recognized as a confrontational manner. Showing off one's knowledge or sharing an unwanted observation, *however well intentioned these things might be*, can sometimes lead to confrontation. Everybody gets nervous or on edge now and then. There are all sorts of ways that confrontation can be avoided.

A low gurgle had begun from deep within the man, a blend of a growl and the sound of an emptying drain. I listened to this sound as though it might become a coherent answer, even if he was only going to say "Peggy Lee" again, but that's not what happened. What happened was that the sound became more complex. The gurgle continued but it was punctuated by these short bursts of wet exhalation, which I deduced were sneezes, though there was no sign that the unblinking man was sneezing and he did not seem capable of it besides. I did not want to draw unwarranted conclusions. And then it occurred to me: it was Roy who was sneezing!

Roy had sneezed himself awake and he was clutching the sides of his bed and looking all around and believe me he was more surprised than I had ever seen him.

"Roy!" I exclaimed with delight. "Do I have a story to tell you!"

THE EVIL LESBIAN

Monday
The Evil Lesbian drove to the health food store for some coconut milk, but they were out, so she went home.

Tuesday
The Evil Lesbian called a plumber. After a roughly twenty-minute visit, the plumber warned her that it was not wise to flush dental floss down the toilet. The Evil Lesbian had never heard this advice before. After the plumber left, the Evil Lesbian drove to the health food store again, and this time scored some coconut milk.

Wednesday
It rained in the morning but when it stopped, the Evil Lesbian went out for lunch and afterwards returned a couple of books on Balthus to the public library.

Thursday
The Evil Lesbian's phone rang while she was coming out of the shower, but she managed to just get to it before the

last ring. It was a wrong number. Later she told this story to a friend.

Friday
The Evil Lesbian went to the dentist for a regular check-up. She arrived on time. She had zero cavities.

Saturday
The Wrr-lsparii, an ancient and highly sophisticated civilization on an uncharted and unimaginably distant planet, were suddenly wiped out by a cataclysmic chain of volcanic eruptions. At the time the Wrr-lsparii had apparently been on the verge of solving the last remaining problems with their teleportation experiments. There were no warning signs of the disaster, and so thorough was the devastation that there now remains no trace of any life, let alone the Wrr-lsparii: the planet that was once theirs is now a flood of silicate magma and raging smoke. It is unclear to what extent the Evil Lesbian may be responsible.

Sunday
On Sunday the Evil Lesbian stayed home.

UNFALLEN

Some months after my daughter broke off their engagement, my inquiries discovered the little ramshackle place to which poor Ivan had retreated. A cabin in a wood might sound picturesque, but this was shabby seclusion. If he was surprised to see me at his doorstep, with my little ribboned box of jam tarts in my hand, he gave no sign. His sleeves were rolled up in a workmanlike fashion and his beard was just slightly less carefully groomed than formerly. It was with some little difficulty that he made us space to use what might have been a cozy sitting room for its nominal purpose, so filled was it with dolls. Without exception these dolls were all ugly, leering and scowling, and it was in the obvious effort taken to convey innocence in each, with a spot of blush here or bright bows there, that the overall effect was most unsettling. Our stilted conversation took place amid a staring crowd, as it were.

We did not discuss my daughter, or the broken engagement. Nor did we discuss the dolls, apart from a fleeting reference to his "current preoccupation": the phrase must have been mine, for most of his contributions were measured gestures of assent: "yes" and "that is so" and "you are right." I told him about the ongoing decline of a few family friends he had been compelled to meet on one occasion or another. I told him that the gardener's wheelbarrow had finally been found, and all of the unlikely details of how an acquaintance's allergies played a decisive role in solving the longstanding mystery. I told him about the progress on the magnificent bridge whose construction my husband was overseeing, a project that has had many delays and unforeseen problems that have repeatedly frustrated and detained my husband. It is all very trying, I told him, but the bridge will eventually be built and celebrated. "Yes," said Ivan. His voice was small but steady, his hands unmoving on his knees.

Of the jam tarts he took only one polite bite. A crumb hung in his beard. Though it is strange to say, I felt embarrassed for him, what with all of those dolls looking at that crumb hanging there. I wanted to take my handkerchief and quickly wipe it away, but the glassy stare of the dolls also prevented that. Suspended but severe judgment hung in that cramped workroom just as that crumb hung in his beard, prone to fall at any moment.

Our interview lasted no longer than an hour.

Stepping through his uneven doorway, we shook hands. My lungs were taking in more air now that we were out from the view of the many ugly dolls, and it must have made me a little dizzy, for in no other way can I account for what happened next. I hardly like to think of it, and can only countenance it because it is in the past, and the past is the work and responsibility of people other than ourselves, though my memory of it is imperfect. I must have taken a step, crouched down, and taken hold of the loose stone, but I can't think when I might have noticed it there. And then I struck him with that stone. Once, ferociously, just above the ear. By the time he had hit the ground I was already walking away, up the path from which I had come, without looking back.

Nowadays my daughter brings her sons to visit by crossing over the celebrated bridge whose construction my husband supervised, while I do not venture very far in any direction. So you see, I have never seen the bridge, let alone actually crossed it.

VISITOR

Some afternoons, when the Red Sox are playing on television, I look to my left and find a man sitting there. He is younger than I and looks at me when I look at him. The same expression is always on his face, regardless of how the Red Sox are doing or what expression might be on my own face. It is difficult to describe this expression of his, but it is not unfriendly. All the same it is unsettling. When the game is over he is not there. Even the armchair in which he was sitting has moved back across the room. Not once have I ever caught him in the act of arriving, pulling the chair over next to mine, and sitting down, and not once have I ever noticed him taking his leave. Sure, I get pretty focussed on the game when it's on, and I sit close with the volume turned up because these eyes and ears aren't the precision instruments they used to be, but all the same it's getting to be a little unsettling the way I turn my head just to the left at some point in the game and there he is, and a little later on, there he isn't. And I am not a man who is easily unsettled.

I rehearse things I intend to say to him, directly to him, the next time he materializes. These tend to run longer than

I first supposed, the more I rehearse them. They grow more elaborate, more finely tuned, because I want very much to express myself clearly, cogently, and fully. Yet the timing of it is at least as crucial as what I intend to say. It wouldn't do to thrust out my words like a challenge, apparently from out of nowhere. So supposing the next time the Red Sox are on television and some great play is made in the game, a slider barely taking second, and I were to turn to the man on my left and observe, "Now that was a terrific steal," and were the man on my left with his not unfriendly expression to say something in return, something simple like "It sure was" or something contrary like "That umpire needs to be retired yesterday, he was out" or even something that might seem unrelated like "All the sorrows of this world," then I would certainly seize that opening and steer the newborn conversation to what I intend to say to him.

What would I say? Well, that too depends on how things get started. It could be simply a matter of whether the Red Sox are winning or not. They don't play half as well as they used to, there's no denying that, but I suppose that's neither here nor there, and besides this man is younger than I am and he may not know his Sox history. But I might say to him, "If this is about Australia, you might as well leave, just give up this routine. You'll get nothing out of it. Believe me, others have tried. It's not up for discussion. It's in the past and it's not going anywhere." But I would only try that tack if there were some sign in his face or in how he responded to my opening sally about the game, something that indicated some interest in Australia.

Or, no less straightforward, I might say, "Look, I'm not

the man you're looking for. I get mistaken for him every now and again. It's not what you want to hear, I know, because you've probably put in a lot of time and effort following tips and leads and now you come here when you know I'll be here, watching the Red Sox on television, and you sit here studying my features, pretending to watch the game, wondering if those features could be, after all these years, the features of the man you've been almost fanatically trying to track down. And so I know you don't want to hear it, but you need to hear it: the man you have found is not the man you are looking for. Now perhaps we can just watch the remaining innings with only one illusion, the illusion that the Red Sox might reclaim their early lead and win this game." It's an earful but he might deserve it. And that would be that.

Still, it's hard to say whether that's the right approach. Mentioning Australia right off the bat, no pun intended, might inadvertently muddle things, if that's got nothing to do with what he's after, and by the same token bringing up the idea of obsessively following leads and tips might be mistaken. If there's one thing I'm not, it's paranoid. I have enough other things to worry about without that. Strategy is essential in life as in baseball, strategy and patience. "Let the ball come to you," I have caught myself saying to the television, as though those highly paid and extensively trained athletes have never before heard this golden bit of advice. It's the kind of thing you say to a kid, just learning to play catch: "Let the ball come to you." And truth be told it's not exactly the most profound advice ever heard, but in fact something of a lie, since the ball doesn't as a rule come to you. It's not passivity that wins the day, that's for sure.

So there's a necessary balance that needs to be struck. Struck, as in struck out, that's getting too close to another baseball pun, but maybe levity is just the thing: maybe a lighthearted approach can take care of everything. "Now there's a funny coincidence," I could say. "The Red Sox are playing and you're here again, and I'm here again, both of us on cue. We must be some devoted fans, you and I, though maybe saps is the more correct term. A couple of saps, letting the air out of an afternoon." Perhaps that might open him up. If that's what's wanted. Now that's just wonderful: bad enough to have to wonder what he's after, I have to wonder about myself, too. That's not how you catch the ball.

For that matter, one's own senses can probably be called into question, not being the reliable entities they once were. "You, sir," I might admonish him, "are a patent hallucination. Every time I try to enjoy a ball game here, sitting up close to the television not disturbing another soul, you appear beside me. The mind is a devilish thing, full of tricks and misfires. You don't speak because you can't. You are probably the effect of cathode rays, something my eyes project when I turn away from the screen too abruptly. I don't know why I'm even talking to you. I'm talking to myself." There's a thought offering no comfort. A damaged mind, a decline of the faculties, what multicoloured joys age brings.

Though not everything is to be chalked up to age. Years ago, many years ago, I was involved in an accident, a car accident. It all happened very quickly and I don't really remember anything about it. Impaired memory, straight up. But what makes me think of it just now has to do what I do remember most vividly. When I woke up in the hospital, after the accident, there was this nurse there, examining me, looking straight at me. And it seemed she was always there. I don't mean that she was some sort of object of erotic fixation or anything like that, you know, and she wasn't attractive at all, just plain, somebody you probably wouldn't really notice in some other situation. But she became this form of consistency, a kind of feature of life, all while I was going in and out of consciousness during that time in the hospital. Eyes open, nurse; eyes closed, oblivion; eyes open, nurse again; and so on. I don't remember her saying anything, and can't recall her voice at all: maybe she never spoke a word to me, but she was always there.

"What do you make of that, hallucination? Can you claim to be any more substantial than that nurse? Or, come to that, to any of those players, tricks of light that I talk to, though they can't hear me off in Boston? Everyone and everything around me might be some kind of transmission or projection. Sources unknown, agendas unknown." Maybe a smile, pretend to be deranged. Or moderately so, deranged but capable of unexpected, cold reasoning. "Like that runt she said was mine, my doing. Well, I know that other people can hallucinate, too, and several in my own experience have shown as much. I can only be tricked so many times. I'm no sap. And no, of course, I'm not perfect, and I've made mistakes. And paid for them, I mean look at me here. There are only so many mistakes a man can pay for, right?" Limit the anger. "Only so many mistakes. Even hallucinations ought to be able to understand that."

I rehearse and rewrite these things that I mean to say,

when the opportunity arises. It's all about choosing the moment. And settling on a strategy. "I confess, I'm old" — drawled out, to seem uncertain, and then flash all resolve — "but that doesn't mean I have to lose my senses, does it? Or lose my nerve? Start believing in ghosts, if that's what you're supposed to be? A ghost haunting me but only during Red Sox games? What does baseball have to do with your haunting me, with what has happened in the past, whatever moment created you, ghost?" Wait for an answer. Patience: don't rush. That's not how you catch the ball. "A ghost of somebody I used to know? Or somebody I never knew but somehow hurt or wronged? Or are you some ghost of the future, what's the word, a premonition? You don't look like any of those to me. You just look like somebody who hasn't yet wised up, who thinks the world is ahead of him, who thinks the world is like a baseball game, and that you might just be able to turn it all around in the bottom of the ninth. That's what you look like to me, sitting there, waiting for me to say something to you, wanting me to explain things to you. Like I should tell you, a person like you, all about Australia and what happened to the money, or the accident, or Yvonne, or all the dirty tricks of this world. As if I remember every detail of all that, as if any of it matters now, after all this time, as if I would tell a sap like you. Haunt somebody else, ghost, there's no future in this."

And I would turn back to the game, satisfied, maybe, though of course not satisfied with the game. Whatever happened to teamwork, whatever happened to winning? Still the game stretches on, always talking about stretches in baseball, though maybe that's because so much of the actual movement of the game seems to be taken up with stretching to get ready for other movement, in case it happens, in case it becomes necessary. But always the game ends, and there's a hand on my shoulder, just barely on my shoulder, and it's time to go.

ACKNOWLEDGMENTS

Any writer might well wonder whether it's easier to ask for permission or for forgiveness. A list of acknowledgments like this one is something like having it both ways. I owe some combination of thanks and apologies to each of the following good and talented people: Stephen Cain, Alisa Cunnington, Adam Dickinson, Jason Heroux, Victoria Lévêque, Erika Mihálycsa, Stephen Remus, and Caroline Szpak. And even more of the same to Clelia Scala.

Some of these fictions have previously appeared in literary journals: *Joyland* ("Society and Others"), *The Danforth Review* ("Broken Pangolin" and "Behind the Scenes"), *Tracer* ("After School Special"), *Flapperhouse* ("When the Seals Would Clap No More"), *Monkeybicycle* ("Shy"), *The Opiate* ("Her Feet"), The Molotov Cocktail ("Transcendental"), and the late, lamented *Numéro Cinq* ("Six Dreams of Natural Selection," which also appeared in Hungarian translation in *Tiszatáj*). My thanks to the respective editors of those journals.

The epigraph from Montaigne comes from Donald M. Frame's translation of *The Complete Works*.

Again I am both fortunate and thankful to work with Rolf Maurer and New Star Books.

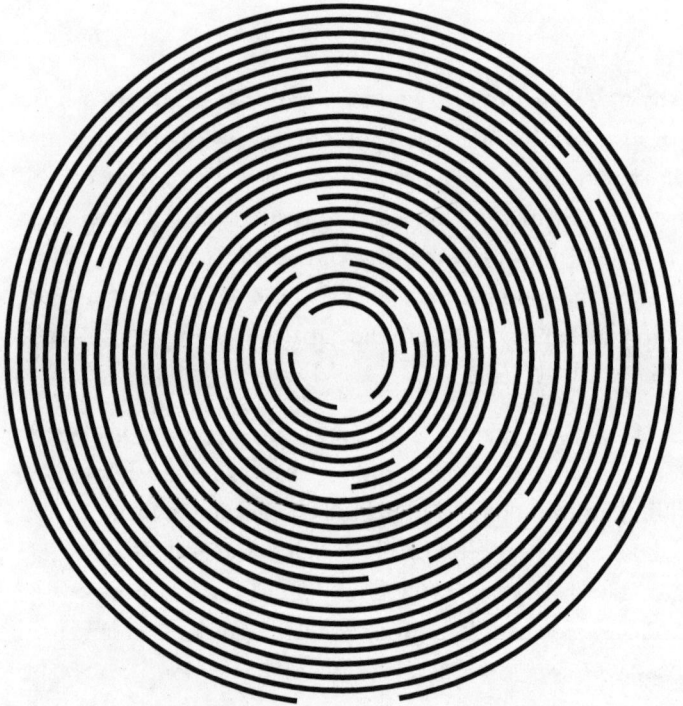